SYMPOSIUM

SYMPOSIUM

MURIEL SPARK

AVON BOOKS NEW YORK

AVON BOOKS
A division of
The Hearst Corporation
1350 Avenue of the Americas
New York, New York 10019

First Avon Books Trade Printing: May 1992

AVON TRADEMARK REG. U.S. PAT. OFF. AND IN OTHER COUNTRIES, MARCA REGISTRADA, HECHO EN U.S.A.

Printed in the U.S.A.

OPM 10 9 8 7 6 5 4 3 2 1

. . . the affair even ended in wounds and the party was finally broken up by the shedding of blood.

Symposium (tr. Loeb: *The Carousal*) of Lucian

. . . the chief thing which he remembered was Socrates compelling the other two to acknowledge that the genius of comedy was the same with that of tragedy, and that the true artist in tragedy was an artist in comedy also.

Symposium (Jowett translation) of Plato

'THIS is rape!' His voice was reaching a
pitch it had never reached before and
went higher still as he surveyed the
wreckage. 'This is violation!'

It was not rape, it was a robbery.

He was Lord Suzy; his title was hereditary, so
that when this was explained to busy people before
their meeting him they were inclined to say, 'Yes,
but what about him?' It is true that he had done
nothing very much. He was approaching the
dangerous age of fifty, said to be the time of the
male menopause. His two previous marriages and
divorces had passed like the storms of old sea-
voyages.

Helen, the present Lady Suzy, was twenty-two.
She stood there sleepy and leggy with her hands
up at her short dark hair, amazed. She had been
married to Brian Suzy nearly a year, during which
she had frequently thought of flight. She had met
her husband at the school play where he had come

to watch his daughter act in *Death of a Salesman*, the dramatic society's choice for that year. Helen was a schoolmate of Pearl, Lord Suzy's only child and from his second marriage. Pearl was now far away in Manhattan operating a word processor at the United Nations and had written about her 'honey of a job', which made Helen feel lonely and envious. Helen's own parents were divorced. She had missed her father most of all, and that, she said, was probably why she was attracted to older men, and had finally fallen for Brian Suzy.

Helen was still standing distractedly among the wreckage, and the two policemen who had woken them in the middle of the night to tell them their front door was wide open with the front-door lights on, now wanted to leave. They were full of wonder that neither of the couple had heard a sound.

'Looks like they made a noise, though,' said one of the policemen.

Helen dropped her hands from her head. 'I heard a noise and I didn't,' she said. 'At least I dreamt a dream in which there was a noise, so I must have worked the real noise into my dream.'

'Now she tells us,' said Brian. 'First she says she didn't hear a thing and now she heard it in a dream.'

'Makes no difference,' said the other policeman. 'Just as well you didn't come down. Might have got bashed.'

When they had gone Helen looked for something intact among the broken bottles. She found some port. In the kitchen where the vandals had not penetrated was a cupboard which contained various bottles of drinks; she pounced on a bottle of brandy, and mixed up her latest-learned brew.

'Brian!' she called. He was sitting at the bottom of the staircase with his head in his hands. She brought him a glass of the port and brandy, her mixture, and sat down on the stairs beside him.

'Rape,' he said. 'It feels like rape.'

'Does it? – I wouldn't know,' she said. 'They took the silver, they took the hi-fi and the Georgian mirror. Then they wrecked the rest.'

It was a Victorian house of three storeys in a quiet street off the Camberwell New Road.

'Robbery,' he said, very much more quietly than when he had first met the shock.

'Haven't you ever had a robbery before?' she said. They had not been long enough married to know each other's detailed histories.

'No. I've lost things. Dishonest servants away back in the past. Inside jobs. My mother lost a ring, too. But I've never been robbed like this. Two-thirty, three, in the morning, and I didn't hear a thing. You didn't hear a thing, not actually. They could have come up and killed us.'

'We should have a burglar alarm,' she said. 'We have to get one. But they know how to de-activate alarms.'

'It's madness to keep silver,' he said. 'A lot of work and in the end they steal it.'

'It was mostly my wedding presents from my family,' she said. His silver was upstairs in a large safe in his bathroom.

'I hate wedding presents,' said Brian. 'If you had my experience of wedding presents you would feel the same.'

'It's true they don't seem to keep marriages together,' she said.

'What's this stuff we're drinking?'

'It's called jumping juice,' she said.

'They've pee'd on the walls, you know,' he said. 'It's so awful when they pee on walls and all over your stuff. An outrage.'

The hostess introduces the people who have not met before. 'Lord and Lady Suzy, that's Brian and Helen, I want you to meet Roland Sykes; and Annabel Treece you already know. Oh, Ernst, lovely to see you . . . Ernst Untzinger . . . You've met, oh, good. Ernst, do you know Mr and Mrs Damien, William and Margaret . . .' The host dispenses the drinks. They are a party of ten. The house is in Islington. The room is very beige, with a glimpse of the dining-room which is predominantly kingfisher blue.

The women in the party are extremely diverse, the five men more similar, although they vary in age. The hosts are Hurley Reed, an American painter in his early fifties, and Chris Donovan, a rich Australian widow in her late forties. They live together. It is a union of great convenience and contentment.

Half an hour later the party is seated at the table. Some are new to each other but on the whole the pair of hosts and their eight guests are far better known to each other than they are, at present, to us.

Hurley Reed sits at the head of the table at this dinner for ten with Helen Suzy on his right and Ella Untzinger on his left. At the other end of the table the hostess, grand-looking and rich Chris Donovan, is already having her attention occupied by Brian Suzy who sits on her right. His dark eyes start out from his thin, dark face. 'They pee'd', Brian insists, 'on all the walls.'

Ernst Untzinger, bronze-faced and successful, with hair greying before its time, is placed on Chris Donovan's left. He has arrived in London on one of his many official trips from Brussels where he sits on one of the international commissions of finance for the European Community. His wife Ella is directly diagonal to him, beside Hurley Reed.

'Pee'd all over the place,' says Brian Suzy.

Ernst is anxious to get him off the subject, since dry champagne is being served in tubular glasses; he feels the details of Brian Suzy's robbery are entirely out of place.

The manservant, not long acquired from the Top-One School of Butlers, assisted by a temporary hand, a young graduate in modern history, is moving round the table, both in their white coats, serving quite impassively, but Ernst is troubled that they should overhear this talk of Lord Suzy's, and shows himself altogether relieved when Brian Suzy goes on to list the actual goods missing and damaged.

'I always say to Hurley', says Chris Donovan, 'that every time you turn your back on your stuff you should say goodbye to it. You never know, you may never see it again.'

Margaret Damien is a romantic-looking girl with long dark-red hair, a striking colour, probably natural. She says, 'There's a poem by Walter de la Mare:

Look thy last on all things lovely
Every hour . . .'

Hurley Reed now raises his champagne glass: 'I would like us to drink to Margaret and William and their future.' William Damien smiles. Everyone toasts the newly married pair.

Hurley Reed, at his end of the table, is now conversing with Helen Suzy on his right. Helen looks uncomfortable since it is impossible to avoid hearing her husband's list.

'That was last week,' says Helen.

'Rape,' comes her husband's voice. 'It felt like rape.'

Helen looks at the plate of salmon mousse that has been softly and silently placed before her. She takes up her fork.

Hurley takes up his and, while passing the tiny rolls to Ella Untzinger on his left, continues his conversation with Helen Suzy. 'Have you ever heard', he says quietly, 'of St Uncumber?'

'Saint Un-what?'

'A medieval saint,' he says, 'to whom people, especially women, used to pray to relieve them of their spouses. She was a Portuguese princess who didn't want to get married. Her father found her a husband. She prayed to become unattractive and her prayer was answered. She grew a beard, which naturally put off the suitor. Her father had her crucified as a result. She's depicted in King Henry VII's chapel in Westminster Abbey, with long hair and a full beard.'

'I'd better not pray to St Uncumber,' says Helen, whose husband at the other end of the table could not be hushed, but was continuing to lament his robbery; 'I might', says Helen, 'grow a beard.'

'Not at all likely,' says Hurley.

'Then I might try the Uncumber method,' says Helen.

Ella Untzinger on Hurley's left, though she is talking to young William Damien, keeps her ears on this exchange between Hurley and Helen. Ella is talking to young William Damien without saying very much, for the subject of the robbery prevails, and William has remarked that his wife Margaret had her bag snatched in Florence on their honeymoon. Ella's long fair hair hangs over her face like a wispy veil.

'Rape, like rape!' comes Brian Suzy's voice from the other end of the table.

'Did you go to the police?' says Ella, her ears still fixed on Hurley's seditious St Uncumber.

'Yes,' drawls William, not that he drawls by nature; he drawls now, probably, because he is bored. 'But we didn't get the bag back,' he laboriously points out. 'The documents were the important things. Margaret lost her passport and her Mastercard, we had to go to the Consulate. All that.'

Ella says, 'What a waste of your time on your honeymoon.'

'It was an experience,' William says.

'Yes, but not an experience you would go abroad to look for, not a welcome one, exactly.'

'Hardly.' William looks across at his wife with a slight twitch of panic that says, 'Will she go on like this?' But Margaret isn't looking his way. The woman on his left, Annabel Treece, is absorbed with her other neighbour, Brian Suzy, and his woes. She has a high forehead, a square jaw. She wears a blue dress with pearls.

'Do you live in London?' William now says to Ella.

'We're often in Brussels for my husband's job but I'm hoping to find a permanent London flat. I've now got a job of my own, teaching at London University. I'm a geographer and a cartologist.'

After all, she is no fool. No one at the table is a fool. Hurley and Chris always give a lot of thought to their guests' level of intelligence when they give a party. William looks more happily towards his wife, who smiles across the table as she lifts a forkful of salmon mousse. She turns her attention to Roland Sykes, the young man on her left. 'Perhaps', she says, 'there's some good in robberies.'

Young Roland Sykes, his carefully silver-greyed hair cut short like a brush, says it is difficult to see what good can come of a robbery unless it be to the thieves themselves.

'According to some mystics,' says Margaret, 'the supreme good is to divest yourself of all your best-loved possessions.'

'There is a difference between divesting oneself and being robbed,' says bright young Roland. 'Leaving apart the utmost moralistic point of view, from any ethical viewpoint being robbed involves some form of crime, whereas the voluntary shedding of one's possessions doesn't.'

Roland's cousin, Annabel Treece, is attempting

to console her neighbour, Brian Suzy, by persuading him that the thieves who had broken into his house were mentally defective, easy victims of drugs, and therefore more to be pitied than blamed.

'Oh, but they knew what they were doing,' says Brian. 'They would have done worse, if only they had known the value of what they didn't take. They left a Francis Bacon on the wall, for instance. They left my wife's guitar.'

'That's entirely my point,' says Annabel. 'What they don't take, not what they take, is significant.'

'Perhaps they felt a picture would be difficult to turn into quick cash,' Brian says. 'And I wouldn't be surprised if they left the guitar out of solidarity with their own generation.'

'Well, the fact remains that obviously they are of rather limited mentality,' says Annabel. 'Or maybe', she says, 'they are history-blocked.'

This puzzles Brian Suzy. Annabel, who is an assistant television producer, is greatly given to philosophical and psychological studies, on which she spends a great deal of her spare time. She has evolved a theory that people are psychologically of a certain era. 'Some people', she now informs Brian, 'are eighteenth century, some fifteenth, some third century, some twentieth. All practising psychiatrists should be students of history. Most patients are blocked', she says, 'in their historical era and cannot cope with the claims and habits of our century.'

'The people who broke into my house must belong to the Neanderthal era,' says Brian. 'They pee'd all over the place.' He speaks testily, even nastily, for he has no mind to make allowances for the robbers, and Annabel herself has no prettiness at all to wheedle a kindlier tone out of him.

The plates are being taken away and the next course is being served. The young graduate helper enters, tall and graceful, dark-locked with a thin brown face, eyebrows that nearly meet and very good grey eyes. He bears a serving dish of plump pheasant, small sausages wrapped in bacon, accompanied by peas and small carrots. Arranging the serving spoon and fork he begins to serve, starting with Helen Suzy. He is followed by the regular butler with a red wine from Bordeaux with which he fills the glasses. The young graduate, having served Helen, moves round the table bending over each of the women in turn. He then, as he has been bidden, serves the men from an identical dish which has been waiting on the sideboard. By the time all have been served with pheasant and wine, the regular manservant has produced on the sideboard a serving dish of sauté potatoes. The timing is as it should be, whether anyone has noticed it or not. But when the sauté potatoes reach Ernst Untzinger, a clatter of the serving fork takes place. It falls to the floor. 'Oh, it doesn't matter,' says Ernst, 'I can use the spoon,' which he proceeds to do. But in reality this little accident has been caused by Ernst attempting to touch the hand of the young man as he serves.

Ella Untzinger is by now talking across William Damien to his left-hand neighbour Annabel Treece, yet not quite excluding him. They have dropped the subject of the robbery and are discussing the question of women's careers.

'I had to have a job. Even married women need a career, everyone knows it,' says Ella to Annabel. 'You, at least, as a single girl, don't have to pick up their pyjamas, brush their suits and iron their shirts.'

'Do you really do all that?' says William. 'I'm jolly glad I got married, if it's true. However, I doubt – '

'It's true more than metaphorically, very often,' says Ella.

Annabel says, 'It's exciting for a woman to touch men's clothes. Psychologically speaking, extremely satisfying.'

'If you love the man, perhaps,' says Ella.

'That, too, of course.'

❯·❯ 2 ❮·❮

THREE weeks before the dinner party at Hurley Reed and Chris Donovan's house, Ernst Untzinger was arranging flowers in the furnished service flat he rented for his visits to London from Brussels.

'Ella', he told the young man who was sitting on the sofa watching him, 'as you know is looking for a flat to buy. She needs to settle in London for her job. I think she will commute between here and Brussels, perhaps even alternating with me. It's rather an interesting situation. Ella loves irises with roses. If you can get them they go very well together.' He had come to the end of what he had to say, but as the young man did not speak, he hummed the beginning of a tune. He then said, 'You know, Luke, Ella and I are really fond of each other. We met when she was sixteen and I nineteen, after all. She comes from Manchester, like me.'

Luke said, 'Ella's a real fine woman. I wouldn't

deny it for the world.' Luke was doing a post-graduate course at London University having graduated from Rutgers in the United States. His home was New Jersey. He had always found his education through grants, and made his spending money by serving at table in restaurants and private houses several evenings a week. He would be serving three weeks hence at the dinner in Islington given by Chris Donovan and Hurley Reed.

A key sounded in the lock: 'Hallo,' said Ella. 'Oh, hallo, Luke,' she said. 'What lovely flowers.' Ella was tall, well-groomed, with her shiny, very fair blonded hair hanging loose about her long face. She had small blue-grey eyes. Her age was forty-two. She was obviously very pleased to see good-looking Luke. She kissed both him and Ernst, who exuded a great deal of good humour on her arrival.

It was Ella who had introduced Luke to Ernst when a few months ago she had asked him to supper in their rented flat; she had met Luke in the university library. Ernst had arrived from Brussels that night. The young man appealed to Ernst, in fact amused him, especially by his way of boasting about some of his perfectly banal academic achievements at the same time as he was positively retiring on the main question about which he could justifiably have put on airs: his courage and independence in putting himself through his universities.

Ernst was tall with partly grey hair, thick black eyebrows, rather glittering eyes so dark that it was difficult to see what colour. He had a good, wide mouth, a newly grown grey beard, a longish nose. It added up to good looks. He was forty-five. He had thought at first that Luke was sleeping with Ella during those odd days and weeks when she came to London on her own, leaving him in Brussels. He had not greatly minded since he had thought it would be, anyway, understandable. Now he thought it only, barely, possible that Luke could be his wife's lover since the young man showed such a decided disposition towards himself.

'We should be careful not to spoil him,' Ella said when Luke had become a very constant visitor, especially during her husband's absences.

Ernst said, 'Don't give him money.'

'I won't. He hasn't asked for any,' said Ella.

'Good. Give him a drink, a meal, it's quite enough. Let him lay the table and wash up.'

'He generally does that. I'm hoping he'll help me to look for a flat.'

Ernst and Ella had one child, a daughter, recently married and now living in New York. Luke was, in a way, filling the gap that she had left. Ernst, so clever, so good at languages, with his Continental connections, preferred his life in Brussels, but since Ella had determined to follow a career in London he was fairly happy to see Luke on his London visits which sometimes lasted as long as a week. Fairly happy the first month of their meeting and now, at the end of the second month, he was becoming strangely delirious. The old madness, the old excitement was affecting Ernst, all he did and thought, there lurking at the back of his mind: young Luke; at those serious meetings and conventions, at those private business lunches: young Luke. I am mad about him, mad, thought Ernst, slashing on his seat-belt and driving away from Heathrow through the traffic towards Luke, with Ella there also, in and out of the furnished flat: 'What lovely flowers.' Sometimes they telephoned down to room-service for their meal, sometimes they prepared it there in the flat's galley-kitchen and ate it at the kitchen counter.

'Stay for supper,' said Ernst to Luke.

'I can't,' said Luke, looking at his watch. 'I'm booked for a party, helping behind the buffet, eight to twelve.'

'How do you get through your studies with all this evening work?' says Ella.

'I don't need to study much,' Luke said. 'It's enough I attend the lectures. I recall everything. A matter of a good brain.'

'Well, I admire you for doing these jobs,' said Ernst. 'Not all young people would do it.'

'A good brain . . .' mused Luke, admiring his own reflection in the deep pool of his mind's eye.

He was far away from Ernst's moral approbation. He was drinking a beer from a can.

Ella left the room to take off her outdoor things. She came back in her blouse and trousers, having changed into a pair of bright green shoes with four-inch heels. Luke looked again at his watch. 'I have to go.'

'Oh, what a lovely watch! It's new, isn't it?' Ella said.

'Fairly,' said Luke. He kissed her, waved across to Ernst, and left.

Ella took a dry martini. She sat down beside Ernst on the sofa. 'Well!' she said. She leaned forward to arrange an iris better in the vase.

'Well, what?' said Ernst.

'The watch,' she said. 'Patek Philippe.'

'It looked expensive,' he said, tentatively, watching her.

'You should know,' said Ella.

'I do know,' said Ernst. 'And no doubt you know better.'

'You gave him that watch, Ernst.'

'No, I imagined you did,' he said.

'I did? You thought I did?'

'Well, didn't you?' he said.

'Of course not. How could I? Why should I? If he got it from you, on the other hand, I suppose there would be a motive.' Her folded feet in the green shoes with their long thin heels were poised on the coffee table.

'I haven't given him anything, Ella,' he said. 'I wonder who gave him that watch?' Ernst sounded worried. 'Thousands of dollars, it represents wealth.'

'You were hoping I'd given it to him,' said Ella.

'I hope nothing. I only wonder,' said Ernst.

'I was hoping it was a present from you,' said Ella. 'If it wasn't I feel strangely afraid.'

'It wasn't a present from me. I, too, feel a sort of fear. It isn't so much the watch, it's the unknown factor,' said Ernst.

'If you weren't attracted to him there would be no need to be afraid,' Ella said.

'If we weren't both attracted,' he said.

'You, perhaps, more than me,' she said. 'But all the same, I don't want to be involved with danger. Luke plus an unknown rich benefactor is danger. What do we know about him, after all?'

'Oh, we know a good deal,' said Ernst. 'He's awfully bright and he's not afraid of doing humble work to make his living. Quite remarkable in a boy his age. You should ask him, Ella, where he got that watch.'

'I couldn't dream of asking him.'

'I mean in a sort of maternal way. You could do it.'

'Why don't you? In a sort of paternal way.'

'I don't feel like a parent towards Luke.'

'Well, in any case, parents shouldn't interfere, nobody should interfere with a grown man. Luke should be free to come and go without our probing,' she said.

They decided to go out to dinner. Ella put on her street shoes and they walked to a Greek restaurant.

'I met Hurley Reed today,' said Ella. 'He's advising a television company on a film that portrays an artist.'

'They never get it right,' said Ernst. 'It never looks right. Pushing their brush into a palette and patting it delicately on to the canvas, all the while reciting an important piece of dialogue, supposed to be a conversation, with someone who has happened to drop in on them. In the studio. Do you think painters keep open house in their studios?'

'That's television and the world of films,' Ella said. 'One reads, sometimes, of painters who used to be available while working.'

'That was in Henry James. Can't the television make it more convincing? What are they paying Hurley? He's well-off. Doesn't need the job.'

Ella said, 'You know, I don't think money is the driving force, there.'

'Nor do I,' said Ernst, for after all, he was a fair-minded man. 'Not that I admire his paintings. If there are messages in pictures I have got the message. I tell you, Ella, that those flat backdrops like posters – deserted dodgems at the seaside or a wooden impassive nurse standing beside a Red Cross van – remind me of the bureaucratic life. Yet he sells for exaggerated prices.'

'Chris Donovan hypes them up. Of course she believes in Hurley,' said Ella, and she thought, Ernst can't help mixing up the price of a thing with the thing itself.

'Nothing sings, nothing flows. There are only inanimate signs. They blow neither hot nor cold because they can't blow at all,' said Ernst. 'And yet they fetch thousands.'

It was true that Ernst had good taste. He went to auctions and enjoyed the putting of a money value on every work of art. He knew it was the wrong attitude, but he couldn't get out of the habit. He was a Catholic. When he visited the Pope, even then, he couldn't help calculating the Pope's worldly riches (life-proprietor of the Sistine Chapel, landlord of the Vatican and contents . . .). Ernst knew it was a frightful habit, but he told himself it was realistic; and it was too exciting altogether ever to give up, this mental calculation of what beauty was worth on the current market.

By unspoken consent Ella and Ernst were not sleeping together any more. If only she knew whether he had slept with Luke. How promiscuous was Luke? The dread disease. For that matter, if only he knew she had not slept with Luke there would be a break in the tension. As it was you slept with everyone they had slept with for the last ten years. There were contraceptives, but it would be an innovation for Ernst. She thought, you can die of it ten years hence and I don't want to. Ernst thought the same. The trouble was they didn't know Luke, and perhaps Luke didn't know himself.

Thinking of Luke now, Ernst's head swam. No sex, absolutely no sex. Romantic love has changed, but absolutely so. Nobody in their senses can be carried away any more, secure in the simple swallowed pill. Now people watch each other. Ella suspects me. She suspects that I suspect her. We could both be right. It's like that vile practice of watching to see if your wife, your husband, goes to Holy Communion. Now they watch for the contraceptive act.

Ernst began to think of his work. Heads of states and their minions sitting at large round tables with interpreters and bottles of mineral water, having such slow, such slow, conversations. Elementary thoughts.

'Chris and Hurley are planning a dinner in a few weeks' time. I hope you'll be here?' said Ella.

'Yes, I'll be in London next week for a month.'

They walked home. The Greek food they had eaten lay on their stomachs like stodge. They agreed: no more Greek food. Never again.

❧ 3 ❧

It was the first week of October, over two weeks before the dinner that Chris Donovan and Hurley Reed were planning to give in London. Venice was still warm, still crowded at the Rialto Bridge, St Mark's Square and the other main points of profuse attraction. Margaret Damien, so recently Margaret Murchie, and her husband William were on the second week of their honeymoon, the first of which they had spent in Florence. With only a few days left, they were writing postcards as they sat in Florian's over-priced café.

'Venice is a whore,' said William.

'You're not writing that down, are you?' said Margaret. 'It goes through the open post. People can read.'

'No, but it's what I think,' he said cheerfully.

But Margaret became solemn. 'We should think positively,' she said. 'Venice is, after all, unique.'

One of the things he admired about his wife was

her moralistic tendency, and especially her refusal to speak ill of anybody. It was old-fashioned and refreshing. Very unusual and people noticed it.

Margaret came from St Andrews. She was tall, like William – if anything, slightly taller.

'Florence is unique, but you had your bag snatched,' he said, hoping to provoke another piece of sermonizing. When she said nothing, he added, 'Florence is also a harlot, of course.'

'Florence was magnificent, it was sublime.' She spoke as if Florence no longer existed except in their memory.

Her face, arms and legs were honey-tanned. William's skin was darker. Margaret would have been a Titian-haired beauty had it not been for her protruding teeth. She had a melodious voice which made the sentiments she expressed all the more mellifluous. William had good grey eyes and a pleasant mouth. He was robust, not yet fat. She was twenty-three and he was twenty-nine; they had met in London in the fruit section of Marks & Spencer's, Oxford Street, less than four months ago. She had spoken first:

'Be careful, those grapefruits look a little bruised.'

He was enchanted right away, having just broken rowdily with a girl he had been living with for almost two years – and she declared herself amazed, later that evening at about ten past eleven, to find that he knew a couple who were related to a girl she worked with in the office in Park Lane which was the publicity centre for a petrol company. William had a job as a junior researcher in artificial intelligence, the bionics branch. He explained this artificial intelligence: the study of animal intelligence-systems as patterns for mechanical devices, a mixed science involving electronics and biology. She was excited by this, wanted to know more and more. She demonstrated such excited interest in the idea that he thought at first she was putting it on. What attracted her was that the capacity of, say, a cat to concentrate its eyesight intensely on one relevant item, screening out the irrelevant, could be studied and copied by human mechanic processes. The frog, the beetle and the bat – experts in their fields . . . 'And the snake?' she said. 'The snake, too,' he told her. 'We can learn from the snake as a biological prototype for synthetic systems.'

Now they were married and walking round Venice as if they had come out of the picture postcards they had just written.

'It's intoxicating,' she said.

'The smell's awful,' said William.

But in that way of hers that he admired so much, she said something about the smell so as to make it of no account. Something about high tides and low tides, always, over the centuries; William didn't catch what it was she actually said; it was not memorable, but her attitude was really, as always, on the side of light.

He took her round the back alleys and lanes of Venice, away from the canals.

'A friend of mine paints these,' he said. 'He calls himself an anti-Canaletto. No bridges and palaces. He's an American artist called Hurley Reed. Everything he does is very squared off and precise, like photographs. You can imagine what he makes of these houses. Very wooden-looking but somewhat interesting, especially painted under the usual Venetian sky which is the only patch of nature to be seen. He's anti lots of things.'

'I'd like to meet him,' said Margaret.

'Well, of course, you shall. He's a friend of mine. A good deal older, of course. In his early fifties, something like that. He lives with Chris Donovan, another friend of mine and my mother's.'

'Who's he?'

'Chris is a she. She's an Australian widow, very rich. I love Chris, she's a good sort. Everyone loves Chris. You'll meet her, too. They live in Islington. They give wonderful parties.'

'What sort of age is she?'

'Ageless. Maybe forty, maybe fifty. Of course she has the money to preserve her looks.'

'It's the expression that counts,' said Margaret. 'It's the expression that reveals the inner person.'

William experienced a slightly heretical or treacherous cloud of a thought: Can I keep up with all this goodness and honeymoon sweetness of hers? So pale honey-yellow and pale moon-grey in tone. I'm bound to put my muddy boots on the vast soft carpet of her character. One of these days, I'll err . . .

He took her on a *vaporetto* to see some Tintorettos, to see Giorgione, to marvel at the mosaics. She was so carried away by the famous *Assumption* in the Frari that it was on the tip of William's tongue to beg her not to levitate.

But it seemed to him it was only in art that their minds really differed. Her moral charm, to him, exacted a small price: she liked art to have an exalted message whereas if there was anything he hated in art, as in life, it was a sermon. She bought a Venetian doll for herself and a toy gondolier for him. It made him feel cosy.

When they were home from their honeymoon, one of the first letters they opened was an invitation from Chris Donovan and Hurley Reed, to dinner on the 18th of October.

William rang to accept and asked Hurley Reed to come in for a drink soon, and meet Margaret. Which Hurley did, the next evening.

Margaret had filled the sitting-room with autumn leaves from the florist. She was wearing a longish green velvet dress with flapping sleeves. Hurley was wondering what she had to pose about in that pre-Raphaelite way. To his astonishment William was apparently besotted with his bride.

She was the sort of girl who made Hurley very homesick for America and a touch of good sense in a woman. What is wrong with her, he wondered, looking at Margaret, that she has to drape herself in green velvet against a background of fall foliage? She could look wonderful in a plain civilian outfit. Why doesn't she get her teeth fixed?

All the time he was thinking this, he was talking.

'We were sorry to miss your wedding. We didn't get back in time from New York. Your mother was there of course,' he said to William.

'Oh, yes, she came.'

'All the way to Inverness?'

'St Andrews,' said the girl.

'Oh, yes, St Andrews. Lovely place. So clear, a beautiful light. And how is Hilda?'

Hilda Damien, William's mother, lived in Australia. She was a friend of Hurley's life-companion Chris Donovan. Hilda, too, was now immensely rich, having made her own money through her own cleverness. Twenty years back she was already a widow of very small means. She now owned five newspapers and a chain of department stores. A magnate, was Hilda.

'She came just for the wedding,' William said. 'And then she flew right back. But she'll be here again shortly to settle about our new flat.'

'I expect you got a fine wedding present?' Hurley fished.

'Yes, exactly that. We got a flat in Hampstead. It's being done up.'

'Good. You're lucky.'

'Aren't we lucky?' said Margaret.

'Hilda's a good sort,' said Hurley.

'Absolutely immersed in the philosophy of *Les Autres*,' said Margaret.

'What?'

'Have another drink,' said William, taking Hurley's glass to fill it with ice, vodka and tonic.

'The philosophy', said Margaret 'of *Les Autres* is a revival of something old. Very new and very old. It means we have to centre our thoughts and actions away from ourselves and entirely on to other people.'

'Oh, meaning the others. Why is it expressed in French?'

'It's a French movement,' said Margaret. 'Well, Hilda, as I say, exemplifies *La Philosophie des Autres*. She really does.'

'Good, well, we'll see you on the 18th. Ten of us, informal.' Hurley left half of his drink, and William saw him to the door.'

'Isn't she wonderful?' said William. 'An amazing sweet character. Do you know where we met?'

'Where?'

'Marks & Spencer's. I was buying fruit. Do you know what she said? – She said, "Be careful, those grapefruits look bruised." And so they were.'

'Good luck,' said Hurley Reed.

❧ 4 ❧

'I DON'T give it a year,' said Hurley Reed. He was referring to William Damien's marriage.
He was dining alone with his Chris, after visiting the Damiens. Chris wanted to know more. 'Who are the Murchies? She was a Miss Murchie.'

'Who knows?' said Hurley. He told her what he thought she really wanted to know. 'Quite nice looking, but terrible teeth, they quite spoil her. I think she's shy or something. There's something funny. Her get-up wasn't natural for a young girl at six-thirty on a normal evening. She had green velvet, a wonderful green, and a massive background of red and gold leaves all arranged in pots.'

'Maybe, knowing you're an artist, she thought you might want to paint her?'

'Do you think so?' Hurley pondered this seriously for a while. 'People do have crazy ideas about artists. But surely not . . . Oh, God, you would have thought she'd have more confidence, because William's highly, deeply, broadly, narrowly, every direction, in love with her. She seems very positive, thoughtful but sunny and agreeable. A mixture, in a way.'

'Why don't you think the marriage will last?' said Chris.

'I don't give it a year,' he said. 'Something tells me. Perhaps it will be more on his side than hers. He perhaps won't make the break but I feel it will come from his side. There's so much money there, besides.'

'Hilda doesn't hand it out to her children. She settles them in life then lets them get on with it. Very sensible.'

'She's bought the couple a flat in Hampstead.'

'I know. It's a wedding present. But nothing beyond that. She told me on the phone; she said, let them work like I did.'

'A good idea.'

'Did they thank you for our candelabra?' said Chris.

'No. Perhaps she hasn't had time to sort out the presents and write, and so on.'

'The young never write,' said Chris. 'They never thank. But it shouldn't depend on her alone. William should thank, too. What's wrong with him?'

'They're just back from their honeymoon. Give them a chance,' he said.

'But the name Murchie,' she said. 'I'm sure I've

heard it before in connection with some affair, some case in the papers; something.'

'Me, too,' he said. 'It'll come to us sooner or later.'

They went into the sitting-room for their coffee, sinking together into the beige downy cushions which were part of their domestic intimacy. Chris had in her hand some notes about their forthcoming dinner party, to which, as always, they were giving great thought.

'Now the Suzys have accepted.' she said. 'The Cuthbert-Joneses couldn't come, they'll be at Frankfurt the whole month. Maybe just as well. So I phoned the Untzingers. She's almost sure they'll both make it. We'll know by the middle of next week. If not, we can think again. Anyway, Ella fixed us up with that student of theirs to give us an extra hand.'

'Who else is certain?' said Hurley.

'Roland Sykes.'

'Ah, the melancholy gay.'

'But he's very good at a dinner,' she said. 'You can put him next to a tree and he will talk to it.'

'And the rest?'

'That leaves Annabel. She thinks she can come. You know she wants to do a feature about you some time in the early spring. I know it isn't like American television but Annabel's show counts, it does count.'

'Sure, it counts.'

'She's intelligent, too,' said Chris. 'In fact we've got an intelligent party, especially if both the Untzingers can come. I thought we would start with salmon mousse.'

'Not salmon mousse,' said Hurley.

'What then?'

'Can't we think of something original?'

'You think of something original.'

'I've been working all day in the studio. I've hardly got the paint off my fingers. What have we got a chef for?'

'Oh, do we really want to leave it to him?'

'I suppose not. Him and his *nouvelle cuisine*. Nobody feels satisfied when they've eaten his tomatoes made into tulips and his wild asparagus made into Snow-White's cottage.'

'I thought we could have pheasant with the trimmings, then salad, cheese and *crème brûlée*.'

'That sounds delicious. I only think it's not original enough since we do have Corby in the kitchen, and everyone knows it.'

'I'll think it over,' she said. 'If you have any ideas let me know.'

'Do you know about the philosophy of *Les Autres*?' said Hurley.

'No,' said Chris. 'What does it involve?'

'Well, according to Margaret Damien it's a new French movement based on, I think, consideration for others. Like, I suppose: others first, me second.'

'I've been practising that all my life,' said Chris. 'Haven't you?'

'I guess so,' he said. 'Perhaps I've expressed it in too elementary a way. Maybe there's more to it than one might think.'

'*Les Autres*,' mused Chris. 'Something new.'

'You could ask her about it,' Hurley said, 'on the 18th. She says that Hilda Damien is immersed in it.'

'Hilda?'

'Yes, she said Hilda's taken it up.'

'What absolute rot. Hilda doesn't take up philosophies and ideas. She's a very busy active woman. The girl must be mad.'

It is the 18th and it seems to Hurley Reed that the dinner is going well. Pheasant seems to have been a good idea, after all, although Hurley had feared it would be boring. Chris had pointed out that it all depended on the quality of the pheasant, and how it was cooked.

Many were the ideas for this course put forth by Hurley and Chris on those evenings, in those few weeks, before the party, when they customarily discussed whatever concerned their ordinary lives. They could have been eating *aiguillette de canard*, consisting of long, very thin slices of duck in red berry sauce, with peas and braised celery. Served with Côtes du Rhône.

But they are eating pheasant, and Hurley notes that the party is going well. For an artist (or possibly this is an integral part of his special type of artistic nature), he is scrupulous about the treatment of his guests when he entertains them to dinner. He dresses well on such occasions: a velvet coat and dark trousers. Chris Donovan loves entertaining with all her heart. It isn't often that Hurley can spare the time but, once he has put aside an evening, he plans it well in advance. They talk about it, over and over, the two of them, till they get all the details right. And so there is always a special sort of lustre – it is not quite an honour, indeed it is almost something finer and sweeter – attached to an invitation to dinner with Hurley and Chris.

Chris Donovan says to Ernst Untzinger, on her left, 'Ask Margaret about the new philosophy of *Les Autres* that she's keen about.' It is a good excuse to get Ernst to talk to Margaret Damien, his other neighbour.

Hurley now is involved with Ella Untzinger, on his left, whom he suddenly finds is charming. She has that upside-down type of mouth, so that if you were to picture it the other way up, the lower lip would smoothly smile upward, while the upper would wavily fit in place: with Ella, all is reversed, and Hurley, like many others, finds it enchanting. Helen Suzy, on his right, is now chatting merrily to her neighbour Roland Sykes, not that that will get her anywhere, Hurley imagines. However Hurley continues, with fascinating Ella, the conversation already inaugurated with Helen Suzy.

The subject is marriage. Forget St Uncumber. Go on to something else, on the same lines, for Ella has been following the talk between Hurley and Helen Suzy about marriage in general, and, in fact, Hurley can't very well change the topic.

'And you,' he says to Ella while the pheasant once more goes on its rounds, 'what are your views on marriage?'

'Well,' says Ella, 'I'm a Catholic.'

'Which means that marriage is final?' says Hurley.

'I'm afraid so.'

'Why are you afraid?' Hurley enquires. 'You should fear nothing if you're a Catholic. Otherwise, what's the point of being a Catholic? My dear Ella, I speak as a Catholic myself. I can't agree, and I speak as a Catholic, very much so, that marriage is final.'

'How do you work that out?' says Ella. She is clever, and knows that any challenge to the Catholic religion has to be absolutely worked out.

But Hurley, now helping himself, last man of the ten, to a second piece of pheasant, has thought well on this subject. He himself has never married. Partly because of his own temperament, partly because his beloved Chris Donovan, for family and tax reasons, never wanted to be married. Hurley gives Ella the fruit of his thoughts:

'The vows of marriage', says he, 'are mostly made under the influence of love-passion. I am talking of modern marriages where the partners have been free to choose for themselves. They are in love. I am not talking about arranged marriages where the parents, the families, have combined to bring about the union. Good. We have a love-match. Let me tell you', says Hurley, 'that the vows of love-passion are like confessions obtained under torture. Erotic love is a madness. Neither of the partners know what they are doing, saying. They are *in extremis*. The vows of love-passion should at least be liable to be discounted. That is why it is possible, and in fact imperative, for a Catholic, who is supposed to belong to the most rational religion, to believe in divorce between people who have been in love, the marriage vows being made in a state of mental imbalance, which amorous love is. There is a reservation, under Catholic laws of annulment, that allows for madness.'

'You mean,' says Ella, 'you should be able to obtain a divorce on the grounds that you were madly in love with the spouse?'

'That's what I mean,' says Hurley.

'I never heard that before,' says Ella.

He nearly says, very pompously: 'Ella, my dear girl, in this house you will hear a great many

[44]

things that you haven't heard before.' But he forbears to say it. He says nothing, and leaves a little silence.

She then says, 'Do you think arranged marriages most likely to succeed?'

'Only in some parts of the world. India. South America, maybe. With us, it's all finished. Arranged marriages only work where the parents know best. With us, the parents know nothing.'

'I agree with you there,' says Ella.

The menu could so easily have been hot salmon mousse, not cold, followed by that thin-sliced duck, or lobster on a bed of cabbage with raspberry vinegar, which were among the many ideas for food that Chris and Hurley had discussed over the past weeks. This homely pheasant in preference to thin-sliced duck, their final triumphant choice, is delicious. The pheasant was hung just right. Do all among them appreciate it? Perhaps more than one might expect. 'I'm glad your mother's back in London,' Hurley says to William.

'Yes, she came a couple of days ago,' William says.

'She's busy about our flat,' says Margaret. 'It's wonderful.'

'Your mother's coming in after dinner,' says Chris. 'I spoke to Hilda on the phone this afternoon. She said she'd look in after dinner.'

'Good.'

But Hilda Damien will not come in after dinner. She is dying, now, as they speak.

5

I T had been in September, while the young
Damiens were still on their honeymoon, that
Chris Donovan had heard how the couple had
met. She learned the details from her old friend
Hilda Damien who had come from Australia for
the wedding. Chris and Hurley had been in New
York at the time, arranging a show for Hurley at a
very good gallery in Manhattan.

Hilda on the phone was announced by Charterhouse, the name, believe it or not, of the new
young acquisition from the Top-One School of
Butlers: 'Yes, pass her to me,' said Chris, among
her breakfast muddle of coffee-pot and toast-rack.
She was in bed. It was only nine-twenty in the
morning.

'Now I ask myself', said Hilda, 'what she was
doing in the fruit section of Marks & Spencer's? It's
not that anyone of that type and generation might
not go and buy her fruit there. But, as it happens,
she was staying in a half-board hostel at the time

she met him. What would she want with fruit and vegetables? She said vegetables – actually vegetables. She had her lunch out. Where would she cook, and why? The story doesn't hang together.'

Chris thought of her friend, already at this hour, up and about, sitting at a desk in her London office.

'Come for lunch,' said Chris. 'I have jet-lag. We just got back from New York.'

'I can't,' said Hilda. 'I can't see you this visit. I'm leaving tomorrow but I'll be back in a few weeks' time to see about their flat. That's all I'm giving them. A flat in Hampstead, full stop.'

'It's a big enough "all",' said Chris.

'That's what I say. They should be thankful.'

Chris said, 'I'll be giving a dinner round about the 17th, 18th of October. Will you be here then?'

'I don't know. I'll ring. I don't believe a word that girl says.'

'Murchie, the name Murchie . . .' said Chris, 'it rings a bell. What are they like?'

What the Murchies were like was something Hilda didn't want to discuss. It was not that she didn't trust Chris Donovan, but that she would have found it impossible to explain what she felt. She was a decidedly practical woman, and it wasn't in her to flounder about with words. There had been more than one occasion for her to experience a sensation of oddness in the two days she had seen the Murchies before and after the wedding in

St Andrews. But the wedding itself, all their friends, were entirely conventional and friendly, just what you would expect a wedding to be for a man like her son.

Hilda said to Chris before she rang off: 'Oh, the Murchies are all right. I don't know them at all. On the whole, I'll be glad to get away. Sometimes I think Australia's not far enough.'

'If it wasn't for Hurley,' said Chris, 'I'd be with you.'

Hilda Damien, aged fifty-three, had a well-preserved look which was only possible to people of her age who had surplus energy. It took energy, also stamina, to apply a routine of physical upkeep such as Hilda had adopted as soon as she realized she was going to have a successful life in her long widowhood. Artists, musicians, writers and poets tend to neglect themselves and their appearance while pursuing their burning and fugitive aims. With many types of business people it is different; they know instinctively the value to their trade of having been massaged and pummelled, groomed and creamed and slimmed, and they give great, assiduous, attention to their smart appearance. Hilda had started as a journalist and now, a real magnate, she took it as a matter of course that she should rise earlier than anyone else so as to fit in the manicurist and masseuse, or the hairdresser.

[49]

Her white hair undulated back from her tan-glow forehead, her teeth gleamed, her good bones held up her facial features; she looked like a mild sunset, she had a strong body.

At fifty-three, unbeknown to her children, she wanted to get married again, the only reason for her secrecy in this respect being that she didn't yet know anyone whom she could marry. But she was convinced, and rightly, that she would easily find a man, preferably a widower, rich, suitable, attractive.

Hilda was not a feminist. She was above and beyond feminism. She had no need of a tame husband to help her with domestic chores, she had no domestic chores. She needed an equal, a mate. And she had always been sexually shy, so she knew very little about all that, without being unaware of the power of sexual attraction.

Although she had no idea whom she might marry she had a good sense of how to go about it. She was relieved that William had got married, and, not expecting the marriage to last, thought she should marry before William's marriage broke up.

Hilda had a woman friend who, in the early days of one of her wealthy widowhoods, sat in the lobby of the Excelsior Hotel in Rome with a little dog on her lap. Before long, a man of suitable age and means turned up to caress the little dog and get into conversation with the widow. Hilda's friend didn't look further. She married this man, who was verging on elderly, and remained happily married till he died. She then returned to the lobby of the Excelsior. Another of Hilda's women friends, well on in her sixties and three times widowed, decided to find a husband about her own age. She went to the Bahamas, where she had some property, and soon met a charming business man at a smart cocktail party. He was her fourth husband and they were still married – she, wrapped in a cloud of contentment. These were the sort of examples Hilda had in mind. She felt, reasonably, that it was a matter of focusing one's mind on the possibility: someone would come and fill the screen. Someone, perhaps, on the plane to or from Australia. Hilda had even thought, how nice it would be to meet a future partner at William's wedding.

The Murchies had made a very good, unspectacular wedding for their daughter. They lived in a turreted edifice near St Andrews called Blackie House, with fewer, and more poky, rooms than the outside suggested. The fact that the rooms were so small was, according to Margaret's mother, Greta, a godsend: 'Otherwise we could never afford to heat the place.' Her husband, Dan Murchie, said his family had occupied the place since 1933. He put a strong emphasis on this insignificant fact, as if 1933 was hundreds of years ago.

'Oh, how often', Dan said to Hilda, 'I was a page-boy at weddings! How I remember the satin suits, the tartan kilts. The blond heads of hair at those weddings, the bridesmaids' curls, and our curls – I could show you photographs. Every month or so a yellow satin suit, a pale blue suit! In a way our parents had money to burn. In another way they didn't have a penny.'

'Luxuries, as we would call them luxuries today, were cheaper. Dressmakers were cheap,' said Greta.

Hilda let them speak on as much as possible. It was her habit to let people speak on.

Hilda stayed with the Murchies for one night, before the wedding. Her room was comfortable in a way that was irreproachable. It had the right curtains co-ordinated with the right bedcovers. It had paper tissues and cotton wool. There was a bathroom attached, pale mushroom-coloured with white birds in flight on the tiles. The towels were right. Everything was right. Hilda had just arrived, been shown to her room. Everything was right, including the piece of Dresden china on a shelf, a silly little man with pink breeches playing a violin. What was wrong with these people? Hilda changed her clothes, which wasn't necessary, or should not have been, as she had arrived in a very smart pair of trousers and a woollen jacket. She looked at the bedside books: three paperbacks by Anthony Powell, *The Trumpet Major* by Thomas

Hardy, Palgrave's *Golden Treasury*, three paperbacks by Agatha Christie, one by P. D. James, something by Thackeray, something by Alan Sillitoe. Nothing wrong with that selection, not a hair out of place. Hilda wore a dress and jacket, black with some white, very good and striking. She went down to meet the Murchies. It was seven-thirty in the evening.

For the first time she met Dan Murchie, Margaret's father. He wore tinted glasses and came into the room with that stiff, correct, Jaruzelski walk that we used to see on the television when the Polish news came up.

'Well, Hilda (if I may),' he said, 'what sort of a journey did you have? Sit down. I'm glad you found us without difficulty. What would you like to drink? Whisky, gin, vodka, sherry, anything.'

She asked for a whisky and soda. In came Greta. 'So lovely to see you,' said Greta (in black and white, she also), 'especially now that the arrangements are all made and the worst's over, one can relax. It's the third wedding I've coped with. My two other daughters. Margaret's the third. The fourth is still at school so I suppose we have that to come one of these days. What a pity you couldn't have come sooner or stayed on a bit; we could get to know one another.'

Her husband handed his wife a vodka and tonic, clinking with ice. He took a neat whisky for himself, tossed it back and poured another.

Hilda thought, 'They are quite all right but there's something wrong.' Then she thought, 'Why should I give a damn?' She sat back in her chair, knowing herself to look splendid, and aware, as they must be aware, that she was very rich and altogether an independent person.

'It was all so sudden,' said Greta. Hilda felt she had expected her to say just that. Was there anything to be said or done that everyone else wouldn't say or do? Hilda thought: 'I have been much too successful. I am out of touch. This, obviously, is what ordinary life is like.'

The Murchies made their living out of quarrying granite and other stone. They had a well organized small business about which Hilda had found out before she left Australia. Dan Murchie of Murchie & Sons, Quarriers and Extractors, Mining Equipment Supplied, was about to retire. But the family business was involved in a sub-contractual way with the Channel Tunnel; and Hilda assumed they needed that sort of money which is necessary to make very much more money. If Margaret had not met William casually in the fruit section of Marks & Spencer's, she would have suspected, and without rancour, that the Murchies might be after William's, that was to say, her, money. It was a situation that Hilda could not have it in her to be too sure of, too cynical about. People did fall in love, quite simply.

'You must be dead tired,' said Hilda to Greta.

'No, as a matter of fact, these days you know with the firms ready to take on practically the whole wedding, it isn't so very tiring. They do the flowers, mail the invitations, set out the presents, everything. One only has to supervise. The list of guests is always a problem. Your list isn't so very long, practically all friends of William.'

'As I wrote to you, mine are nearly all in Australia,' said Hilda, sipping her drink. 'However those few who can come – it'll be good to see them.' And she thought: William's first wedding. There will be others.

She had met Margaret in London. She didn't think the marriage would last. That goody-goody type of girl, how could she be real?

Hilda had sat good-humouredly in their too-small flat and chatted as she noticed.

'Marks & Spencer's fruit section. What on earth were you doing there, William?'

'Buying fruit,' he said. 'I always went there, it was convenient.'

'And you,' she said to Margaret in her best Sandringham-type manner, 'was that your favourite fruit shop?'

'No, I was just there by chance.' She gave a little smile, put her head on one side. 'Lucky chance,' she said.

William sat there goggling at his bride-to-be as if she were a Miss Universe who had taken a double first at Cambridge, or some such marvel.

'I shall give you a flat for a wedding present,' Hilda had said. 'That is all I propose to do.'

'Why, it's too much,' said Margaret.

'Very generous,' said William. After all, what could he say?

'My parents', said Margaret, 'are dying to meet you.'

'It's a most exciting occasion,' Hilda had said, holding out her glass to William for her drink to be repeated.

6

A BOUT two weeks before the dinner party, Hurley Reed met Annabel Treece unexpectedly at the television studios. Hurley had been attending a session as adviser for a television play in which an artist was depicted. It was six in the evening. Annabel had just finished her day's work. She was normally a documentary producer. They went to have a drink.

'They are talking about this artist character's retiring,' said Hurley. 'All wrong. Artists don't retire. There's nothing for them to retire about.'

'I hope you told them so,' said Annabel who admired Hurley. 'In a way it's a waste of your precious time, this advisory job.'

'But I like to see them do it right,' Hurley said. 'In this case, for instance, the painter is not perpendicular enough. He shouldn't be shown to look away from the canvas to talk while his hand is painting with the brush. I like things done right. Personally, if I were a butler or a valet I would do it right. I would know how to do it.'

'How would you know?' said Annabel. 'Have you had the experience?'

'Yes, on the employer's side,' Hurley said. 'Since I've been with Chris we've always had a man-servant or two.'

'This is something I'd like to hear more about, for when I do that TV profile of you,' said Annabel.

'I'd rather leave the butler out of it,' said Hurley. 'Quite honestly, for an artist that sort of thing is counter-productive. At the other end of the scale, so is starvation and garrets. If the public thinks you're too well off they figure the art must be superficial, and if you're poor they think there's something wrong with the art, and why doesn't it sell?'

But Annabel was not to be waylaid. She was storing up an idea which she felt would impress her superiors when it came to persuading them to take on her projected profile of Hurley. About the observations he had just made, she was not concerned. (Artist . . . butler . . . maybe include rich Australian consort . . .) 'What's the name of your butler?' said Annabel.

'Charterhouse,' he said.

'I don't believe it.'

'Neither did I,' he said. 'But it's true, it's on all his papers and references. We only just hired him.'

'Is he any good?'

'Perfect. Except he already talks about wanting a few weeks off in the late fall.'

'Did he say "fall"?' said quick Annabel.

'No, he said, "Autumn, sir." He wants time off to take his Greek wife back to Greece where she insists that she has to claim her dowry. I daresay that means twelve sheets, six pillow-cases. They haven't been married long, the fools.'

'Do you think marriage is foolish?'

Hurley ignored this. 'Chris is going to let him go on vacation. But first we're counting on him for a few occasions, including a dinner. After that, let him go to Greece. A small dinner, we thought, rather special.'

'Chris invited me, I was thrilled,' said Annabel.

He enumerated the list of guests, some of whom she hadn't met.

'It sounds charming,' she said.

'They will constitute an interesting cocktail,' Hurley said. 'That's what one asks of a dinner party.'

'And I'm looking forward to seeing Charter-house,' Annabel said.

'Nothing special to see,' said Hurley. He smiled at Annabel and paid the bill for their drinks.

To her cousin Roland Sykes with whom she had supper that night Annabel said, 'I hear you're going to Chris Donovan's dinner party.'

'I've been asked. I don't know if I can manage,' he said, as he always said; to the effect that she took no notice.

'I met Hurley,' she said. 'He told me who's coming. There's a newly married couple; he's the son of that magnate tycoon woman, Mrs Damien, an Australian; you remember there was an article about her in one of the Sunday supplements. Her son got married to a girl called Margaret Murchie from St Andrews. Hurley says they met in Marks & Spencer's, the fruit section.'

'Murchie?' said Roland.

'Well, it's an old Scottish name.'

'I know. From St Andrews, you said?'

Annabel's cousinship to Roland was from the mother's side, his from the father's. They both had brothers and sisters, but Annabel and Roland were much closer to each other than to any other members of their family. Annabel was more than five years his senior. Their devotion dated back to their teens, when he was fourteen, she nineteen. They would have married or been lovers, certainly, had Roland not from his teens been sexually attracted to men more than he was to women. Roland shared a large flat with a busy journalist towards whom he was friendly without further complications; the flatmate always had a girl-friend to stay some nights and all weekends but the spaciousness of the flat made it easy for Roland to avoid them. He felt very comfortable at home. But it was to Annabel that he brought his sorrows and griefs. He had for some years been thinking and deciding whether he should come down, finally, 'on one side' as he put it, meaning that he wanted to give up homosexuality and get married. It was not easy in the sense that it was a course of action easier to decide, and even to attempt to put into practice, than to realize, for he had been known as a homosexual, and the sort of girls he would have liked to marry were not, so far, available to him. These woes he fully confided to Annabel, since there was now no question of romantic love between them. It was too late. Their relationship had set into an abiding family closeness. The thought of going to bed with her cousin Roland would not have pleased Annabel, while for his part, in his present state of mind, he would have thought her too old. They were, all the same, dearer to each other than most cousins, most sisters and brothers, are to each other.

Roland was by profession a genealogist, an honest one, much as he was sometimes tempted to soar into the clouds of mythology to clinch his findings. He worked for a large firm of private investigators whose main activity was spying on lovers and tracing missing people. But a substantial profit was made by Roland's branch of the business. He traced people's ancestry. Mostly those were people who had made a lot of money and who felt they must be, or might be, descendants of some distinguished house or family or person; also, in many cases, they wanted some form of crest and motto to put on their dinner forks and spoons or to have engraved on their signet rings.

Members of the Church of the Mormons or Latter-day Saints were particularly good clients for genealogists in England; from Utah alone came substantial revenues, since descendance from Joseph Smith or one of their enlightened founders was considered by them to be a personal asset.

One way and another Roland was kept busy. He knew where to look for documents, what public record offices, what historical archives and where the papers were kept, what parish registers, throughout the country, and he was familiar with emblems of heraldry, those still flourishing and current and those which were extinct. He was also an excellent paleographer, so that he could decipher the peculiarities of handwriting, spelling and the varying dialects of scribes, clerks, clergy, lawyers, judges and country gentlemen dead long and many centuries since. And he was honest in this: he exploded as many false claims of pedigree as he discovered true ones. But in the process of explaining, not much was in fact quite straightforward: there were areas of doubt. Roland was firm about expressing doubts where doubts existed, and if the clients wanted to give themselves the benefit of the doubt that was their business.

In Annabel's brown and green sitting-room Roland waited for Annabel's dinner to announce itself ready by the ping of a timer bell. He said, looking into his drink and swirling it round, 'Murchies of St Andrews?'

'You know the family?' said Annabel.

Roland, an extremely busy young man, did not normally know families as such. Like specialist doctors he had to consult his records if clients came back saying they had been to him before. He had an efficient computer service at his disposal. But his natural memory usually told him a lot.

'There was something about the Murchies last year. I'm sure it was St Andrews,' he said. 'But of course, the details . . . I'll have to check. I did some research, yes, but there was something else. They wanted to claim a fortune but didn't succeed in the courts, it was all in the papers. It need not be the same family.'

'We'll meet the girl on the 18th.'

'I'm not sure I can go.'

'Oh yes, love, you can go to the dinner. If there's anything nice in this world it's Chris and Hurley's dinners. But I want you there so we can talk about it afterwards.'

Ping, ping, went the cooking bell. Annabel sidled into her kitchen, then called Roland, 'Supper's ready!'

Suddenly he thought: What, what, would I do without Annabel?

She said, 'You've changed your hair-style.' Normally his hair was dark, with a side parting. Now he had it cut brush-like sticking up a little on top of his head, very short at the sides, and silvered.

'It's a change,' he said.

'I wouldn't think it would persuade a woman that you've changed,' said Annabel.

'To a young girl today it means neither one thing nor another,' said Roland.

'It would mean something to me,' said Annabel, 'and I'm not so old.' She was thirty-two, he twenty-seven.

'I'll try it out for a while,' Roland said. 'Maybe you're right. If so, I wonder why?'

'It looks as if you've spent hours and hours at the hairdresser,' Annabel said.

'So I did,' he said.

'And it will grow out quickly. You'll have to spend more hours keeping it up. I don't say', she said, 'that it doesn't look good. It makes you look decidedly attractive.'

'Thanks. I'm glad to know it. I was getting bored with myself.'

'You belong to the eighteenth century,' she said. 'The men were obsessed by their hair and their wigs. You can see by the portraits. Psychologically, you are eighteenth century.'

'You told me so once before. I forget why.'

'It was because I'm eighteenth century too. Basically, my morals are eighteenth century. That's why we get on so well, I think. We've both of us skipped the nineteenth century in our genes.'

7

L ONG before Margaret Murchie met William
Damien in the fruit section of Marks &
Spencer's in Oxford Street – nearly two
years before – she sat with her parents and an
uncle in the cluttered sitting-room of turreted
Blackie House within the sound of the North Sea
at St Andrews. It was a glorious October day; the
light had that angelic radiance of a Scottish autumn
and its tingling freshness, so welcome to people
who enjoy feeling cold, as the Scots so often do.

'What is your advice, Uncle Magnus?' said
Margaret.

Magnus was the only imaginative factor that had
ever occurred in the Murchies' family, but unfor-
tunately he was mad, and had to spend his days
in the Jeffrey King hospital, a mental clinic in
Perthshire from where he was fetched, early on
most Sunday mornings, to spend the day at Blackie
House. Magnus was beyond cure, but modern
medicine had done a great deal to mitigate his

condition. He had a mad look. He was large, and ate voraciously. There had been a time when he was too violent to have at home, but thanks to the pills they gave him he was violent no more. He had always had periods of comparative lucidity, hours and hours of clarity, even days of it. Then, at any moment, he might go off on his ravings.

Many families have at least one fairly mad member, whether in or out of an institution. But the families do not normally consult the mad people even if they have lucid periods; the families do not go to them for advice. The Murchies were different.

Dan and Greta Murchie swore by the sagacity of Dan's elder brother, Magnus. Greta felt he was inspired.

'In the Middle Ages,' Greta said, 'the insane were considered to be divinely illuminated.'

'He's my brother as well,' Dan said. 'He can't be all that mad.'

'And there's a way of willing people to be serviceable,' said Greta. 'You can use your will-power and make what is not so, so. Everyone knows that.'

And Dan contributed a doctrine of St Thomas Aquinas which, like several others of the philosopher's teaching, does not stand up to practicality: Do not, wrote Aquinas, take note of who is speaking, but of what is said take note.

Greta brought to the question a final consideration: 'The nursing home is costing us a lot of money. Let us get something back.' In fact it was Magnus's money which was keeping him in the private clinic, but to Greta and Dan it came to the same thing.

Magnus had now been their guru for six years. He it was who had suggested a course of action which was to cause the Murchie scandal.

He had a vast beard. Wearing a bright blue and satin-silvered windjammer, black leather trousers and elaborate brown leather country boots of a very recent design, with four cross-straps and the name Steiner imprinted on the front, Magnus lorded it over his Sunday outing.

The Murchies' aged mother was now sick in a nursing home in Edinburgh. Mad Magnus and Dan were her only sons. She had three daughters, two of whom were unmarried and decidedly helpless. The third was married and lived in Kenya where her husband had a business job.

Everyone knew that the old and failing Mrs Murchie had left her fortune equally among her five children. She had made it clear. It was a Scottish will, with quaint but decided mention of 'the bairns' part'. The will had been written long ago in 1935 on the death of her husband.

'Out of date,' said Magnus. 'Besides, I don't want my part. It will only go to the Master in Lunacy.' He was referring to the old-fashioned term for Master of the Court of Protection, the present authority whose office deals with the interests of mad people.

'Ah, you might get better,' said Dan. 'You might come out and be normal.'

'I don't want to,' said Magnus. 'It is written, "The Lord shall go forth as a mighty man, he shall stir up jealousy like a man of war: he shall cry, yea, roar: he shall prevail against his enemies." That,' said Magnus, 'is what I cite and it is what I say. See also Isaiah 38: 12, "I have cut off like a weaver my life: he will cut me off with pining sickness." So what I suggest is that you make Ma change her will, cutting me out and the girls, and leaving the lot to you.'

'Easier said than done,' said Dan.

'See the lawyer. Primogeniture is a necessary concept in law when a house has to be kept up. When Ma made that will the upkeep of big houses was an afterthought. If you count me out because of my pining sickness, incurable, you are the only son and the eldest.'

Dan repeated this to his wife Greta. She thought it a good idea that Dan's mother should be asked if she wanted to make a new will, but she did not want to be the person to suggest it. Nobody wanted to suggest it.

'Anything the matter?' said the elder Mrs Murchie.

'No,' said the visiting son. 'Perhaps one or two things we have to discuss some time.'

'We can discuss them after I get home. Next week, they say. Waters came to see me.'

'What did he want?' James Waters was the family lawyer in Edinburgh.

'He came to see me. People do come to visit.'

Dan felt relieved. He had been uneasy at the prospect of approaching the family lawyer about his mother's business. He wanted her fortune, and it was really hers, not inherited from his late father. But Dan also wanted to keep the affection between them afloat. Greta, too, was fond of her mother-in-law and she, too, was relieved to know that the first step toward the elder Mrs Murchie seeing a lawyer had been taken by the lawyer himself, even if the step involved no more than bringing her twelve pink roses to the nursing home.

Dan's mother was to visit St Andrews the following week. She had suffered a heart attack. Her condition now seemed to be under control. Greta was to go and fetch her at eleven in the morning.

But at four in the morning the telephone was screaming beside the bed. 'Perhaps it's your mother. You answer it,' said Greta.

Dan answered it. 'Yes, her son speaking,' said Dan. 'Police?' said Dan. 'Oh, God, right away. I'll come right away. No, I've got a car; yes, perfectly able.' He was hardly able to drive in his state of shock. Greta pulled on her trousers and her woollens and got in the car with him. Mrs Murchie had been murdered, strangled by an escaped maniac, a young woman who had been in a mental home for twelve years, as a secondary result of an irreversible drug sickness; the primary cause of the woman's psychotic state had been a built-in mental defect. There was nothing to be done about the strangler, who was caught without fuss, calmly walking along the road towards the docks at Leith in the moonlight.

But how she had got away from the maximum security wing of the mental home, why she had made straight for the nursing home in Edinburgh where Mrs Murchie lay in her private room, how she had entered this nursing home, and how and why she had gone to Mrs Murchie's room – why exactly Mrs Murchie? – were questions to which the police and after them the press set about to try to obtain answers. They tried in vain, and not for long: 'It's useless', said the Chief Inspector to Dan, 'trying to find a motive when you are dealing with the insane. They are infinitely cunning, they bide their time. Perhaps she was hypnotized. Or perhaps the woman knew, or got to hear, of the Calton Nursing Home and thought she would be better off there, herself, than in the Jeffrey King, and somehow got into a room, any room, and found your mother there, and . . .'

'The Jeffrey King?' said Dan.

[70]

'Yes, that's the name of the clinic near Perth where the woman got out of. A security wing, mind you. Lock and key, it means nothing to them. Cunning. Superhuman strength.'

Dan left it at that. He didn't even tell Greta where the strangler came from; she read it in the papers. The sheriff brought in a verdict of death by strangling at the hands of one not fit to plead. There was not a great deal in the press. One day's horror headline and a report of an enquiry at the Jeffrey King clinic into security measures; that was all.

It was Greta, on the way home after the funeral, who finally said to Dan, not he to her, 'Magnus must be behind it.'

'Well, but why? The way he was talking last Sunday would seem to show that he wanted to keep Ma alive, at least until she made a new will.'

'Funny that the mad woman was in the same home as Magnus. How could she have made her way to Edinburgh, precisely to the Calton Nursing Home and to poor Ma's room?'

They were badly shaken by the horrible affair, but even more so when they heard that Mrs Murchie had indeed changed her will.

'I think I am going mad,' said Dan. What he meant was that he couldn't face the implications. Only Margaret had been with him the previous Sunday when Magnus suggested that their mother change her will.

'Phone Margaret,' he said to Greta. Margaret at this time had a job and a flat in Glasgow. She had just got back from the funeral when her mother got through on the telephone. 'I know she changed her will,' said Margaret. 'I arranged for Waters to go and see her. I was there. I said, "You asked for Waters, Granny, as you wanted to change your will in my father's favour, which I think is logical." Waters fully agreed. She was delighted with the flowers. He had brought a newly drafted will. At first she wanted to divide her property between the aunts and my father, but we said that wouldn't work. Anyway, we amended the draft and Waters took it away. He came back the next day and she signed it in front of witnesses. She was very happy. At least she died happy. Now Dad's quite well off, we can keep the house.'

Greta conveyed all this to Dan and then by phone to her two elder daughters, who were so different from Margaret.

These daughters were not long married. They both had jobs. The eldest, Flora, was an elementary teacher, her husband a junior solicitor; they lived in a house at Blackheath, where they let a flat to help pay up the mortgage. The next younger daughter, Eunice, was married to a personnel manager in a car factory. She taught in a comprehensive school at Dulwich, where they lived. Flora was fairly pretty, cautious, pedantic, with a deep craving for a life of fixed routine which her young husband fitted in with; it didn't matter much what exigencies arose in Flora's life because she could somehow fit them in with a known scheme, an already documented case-history, or under some trite heading. Her husband was helpful in supplying the right language. The murder of her grandmother was 'an unfortunate incident', the fact, with which Flora was presently acquainted, that the will had been changed in her father's favour, was a 'coincidence, fortunate in the circumstances'. That Magnus was mad was something that 'happens in the best of families'. The fact that the homicidal maniac came from the same mental hospital as the one where Magnus was lodged, was just a fact: 'One thing has nothing to do with another.' Flora took her bath, which she always did at night, prepared her clothes to put on the next day, while Bert, her husband, set the breakfast things ready for the morning. Qualmless and orderly, they went to bed.

Her sister Eunice, fair with pale eyes and long hair, was now five months pregnant. Her general outline was vague and fuzzy, like a shakily taken photograph. She said to her mother, 'I hope this news doesn't upset *me*. The murder was bad enough.'

'Perhaps I shouldn't have told you,' said Greta.

'Well, you've done it now.'

'I thought you'd like to know at least that Daddy will be free from financial care.'

'Lucky him.'

'It was Margaret who sent Waters to visit your grandmother. And make her change her will.'

'And Granny was killed the next day?'

'No, three days later. I mean, Waters went back on Friday to get her signature.' Mrs Murchie had died on the Saturday night.

'It looks very fishy,' said Eunice. 'I feel bad about it. Peter won't like it.'

'We don't like it,' said Greta. 'Your father and I feel it looks so bad. But what can we do about it?'

'It was Margaret's idea, then?' Eunice said.

'Yes. Well, no. To change the will was your Uncle Magnus's idea.'

'Oh, God. If the press gets hold of this, there's going to be trouble. It's all so bad, in my condition.'

Jean, the youngest daughter, still at school, had been sent to a convent in Liège the Monday following the fatal Sunday when Mrs Murchie senior was murdered. Greta had been to school in this convent. Jean, a hankerer after adventure, went willingly, quite unaware of the cause of her grandmother's death. It was at Liège, that innocent and beautiful city, that young Jean was to encounter a certain Paul, eighteen years old, son of an old Belgian school friend of Greta's, preparing to be what he himself called a Eurocrat. Eventually Jean was to have a child by Paul and to live lovingly with him year in, year out; but that is another story, or would be but for the mere fact that her destiny was contingent upon the murder of her grandmother and her having been packed off quickly to those faithful nuns at Liège.

Dan's favourite among his children was Margaret. It was a passion that he mutely controlled. Dan could sit for hours simply watching Margaret. Wherever she went, his eyes followed her as far as they could. He watched her reading, marvelling over the bloom of her lovely complexion. He thought her intelligent, too original to be appreciated.

'Someone put that maniac up to killing my mother,' Dan said to Greta.

'It must have been Magnus. It must be,' said Greta. 'They say there was no contact between Magnus's wing and the dangerous cases. That's what they say, it's what they always say, what else can they say?'

'He knew the will had been changed.'

'Someone must have told him,' said Greta.

'Yes, I believe Margaret told him. She rang him up in the home and she said he'd be glad to know the will was changed as he suggested. Apparently, he was delighted. And if Margaret was mixed up in this, I'm stunned,' said Dan.

'I'm not,' said Greta. 'And there's no "if" about it. She sent Waters to change your mother's will in your favour, and then told Magnus. That's being mixed up.'

Margaret turned up that night. She had a few days off from her job as a ceramics designer in Glasgow. Her parents looked at her with fear, in a new way, not quite knowing her for the first time in their lives. Dan said, 'I wonder how Magnus got to know that psychotic woman? It must have been Magnus who sent her.'

'But supposing it wasn't?' said Margaret. 'Aren't you doing Uncle Magnus a great injustice? You have no proof at all.'

'That's what I say,' said Greta, although it wasn't at all what she had been saying.

'And then', said Dan, 'she had only just changed her will, and Magnus knew it.'

'But she didn't change it in his favour,' Margaret said. 'Don't you see, Granny cut him completely out. Nobody could accuse him of killing Granny for her money. They say in the hospital that he's very upset. Won't move out of his bed.'

'Have you been in touch with the hospital authorities?'

'No, the police have. And they were in touch with me,' said Margaret.

'What for?' said Dan.

'About the will.'

'Oh, God,' said Greta, 'the will isn't our fault. It was natural that she should make a new will, wasn't it, after all these years?'

The police apparently thought so, too, or were obliged to recognize that possibility. The official enquiry at Jeffrey King mental home led to nothing but some recommendations for tighter control. There was no trial. The strangler, found unfit to plead as indeed she was unfit to utter any consecutive sense or implication, and more victim than brute, was sent to an institution for the criminal mad. The press went on to more intense and exciting things and would have stopped giving up even a paragraph to the case had Dan's married sister who lived in Kenya not decided to challenge the will. She had flown home for the funeral. She now mobilized her two unmarried sisters in favour of a theory of 'undue influence' having been put on her mother on her sick-bed by the interested party, Dan. There was no way in which they could prove anything against Dan or Margaret. The nurses were in perfect accord that Mrs Murchie had, on her own, asked Margaret to send the lawyer in to see her, and Mr Waters himself insisted indignantly that Mrs Murchie had made a new will of her own volition and while in her right mind. Dan settled the business out of court, as he had in any case intended to do, while the sisters stomped in and out of their late mother's flat in Edinburgh, removing things, assessing things, parcelling them out amongst themselves.

Dan had never had much to say to his mother; he was at a loss. What had affected him at his mother's funeral was the actual sight of her coffin, the sight of that brown coffin, that box. Now, he was amazed at her daughters' looting her goods – her daughters, one of whom had been extremely devoted.

'Surely we should have a say in all this?' said Margaret. 'It would be good to remind them of your rights.'

'Yes, good. But at this particular moment it would look bad,' said Dan. 'Our hands are tied.'

It was the end of October. 'Was it Undue Influence?', 'Magnus Murchie: Nothing Can Bring My Mother Back', went the headlines. An editorial in a more sober paper pointed out that the days of witch-hunts were over. Nothing could be gained by persecuting the Murchie family. Plainly, the murder had not been planned by the interested party, her son Daniel. Equally obvious was it that the will had been changed in the ordinary course of the unfortunate Mrs Murchie's illness: she had not changed her will for fifty years. What more logical than that she would wish to leave her fortune to the son who was of right mind? Her three daughters, who, it was understood, in a prior action decided to contest the will, had now withdrawn their case. The question had been settled out of court. Reasonable people might now agree to leave the Murchies to their grief.

The fuss blew over by the end of the year. Dan developed eye-strain and wore dark glasses nearly all day, even in the Scottish winter. Greta paid up her racing debts; got her brooch out of pawn, and sent cheques to Flora and Eunice, lamenting the fact that their aunts, by contesting their grandmother's will, had 'robbed' them. 'Think how much more we could have done as a family', wrote Greta, 'if those aunts of yours hadn't been so avaricious. Margaret is wonderful. She refuses to touch a penny of her grandmother's fortune. She says she's happier that way.'

The fuss blew over, and two years later, when Hurley Reed and Chris Donovan were planning their dinner party, and various of their friends were discussing the newly married William Damien and Margaret, the Murchies' name was only something a few of them remembered seeing in the papers. Murchie or some name like that. Some scandal, but probably, anyway, not the same Murchies as Margaret's family.

'If there is anything I could not bear to do,' said Margaret to her father, 'it is to profit by darling Granny's death.'

Dan looked at his daughter through his dark glasses, as a rabbit might look at a stoat: dismay, fear, despair. If she had been greedy for her grandmother's money, now her father's, at least he could have understood. But beautiful Margaret was here detaching herself from any blame. But was she to blame? Dan felt, not with his mind, but deeply within the marrow of his bones, that she had sent the maniac to her grandmother.

'Not a penny would I touch,' said Margaret. Dan went cold. He was sure his daughter meant it.

Magnus again came to St Andrews for the Sunday, dressed in his gaudy clothes. 'Let's go for a walk,' said Dan; which was unusual, for it was known he didn't like to be seen with Magnus, dressed like that. Who would? Only Margaret. She didn't care what Uncle Magnus looked like.

They possessed a stretch of woodland, narrow but long. Greta from the window saw them walking between the trees, with large Magnus's bright blues and reds flashing. She thought perhaps it was time, now that the financial side was settled, that Dan gave up Magnus as a guru and a guide. It was weakness on Dan's part; madness. They were not a mentally stable family, those Murchies.

What Dan was consulting his brother about, there in the woods walking along the edge of the dank pond, was Margaret. 'Do you think her capable of murdering Mama?'

'I think her capable of anything,' roared Magnus. 'An extremely capable girl, very full of ability, power.'

'But murder? Provoking a murder? Causing someone else to do it?'

'Oh, that, yes, I dare say.'

'Magnus, this is completely beyond me. It's terrible. She refuses to touch any of our money, now. She won't touch her grandmother's money, not a penny.'

'She is naturally a girl of high principle. I would have expected that.'

'Sometimes I wonder, Magnus, if you advise us right.'

'Who else have you got?' Magnus bellowed. 'Third-rate lawyers, timid little bankers from London. No guide whatsoever for a Scot.'

'Magnus, keep your voice lower. Hush it.'

Magnus lowered his voice. 'Who do you have', he said, 'but me? Out of my misfortune, out of my affliction I prognosticate and foreshadow. My divine affliction is your only guide. Remember the ballad:

As I went down the water side
None but my foe to be my guide
None but my foe to be my guide.'

'Perhaps', said Dan, 'you can't be a friend. Maybe in fact you're our worst enemy. It may be.'

'Undoubtedly,' said Magnus. 'In families, one never knows.'

'What I am wondering,' said Dan, 'is if Margaret is sane.'

'Probably not. Perhaps she inherited something wild from me. Is it time for a drink?'

'Yes, and then I have to take you back, right away.'

8

THERE was probably nothing more pleasant in the whole of London than the charming love between Hurley Reed and Chris Donovan. They were both convinced that marriage would have spoiled everything for them, and undoubtedly they were right. Hurley was nothing like so wealthy as Chris; as a husband he would have felt diminished, the smaller partner; as it was, the question of greater or smaller didn't arise. For her part, Chris felt younger not being married, she had been married and had got used to always having a man to keep her company and talk to, but now she was a widow, and rich, she really enjoyed the single-woman feeling, with Hurley as a companion. She found him very entertaining. He depended on her a great deal for the material props to his career; after all, he was not a great artist, he was in a way too much of a thinker to be a true and full-blooded painter, not that he was a big thinker, either; he was an interesting man with some talent. His liaison with Chris had lasted seventeen years, and was still doing very well at the time of the dinner party they were planning, the latest of so many dinner parties they had planned and given.

'Do you remember', said Hurley, 'that dinner we gave, something like – it must be fifteen years ago, when that girl got up at the end of the meal and raised her hands to heaven, invoking the Lord to bless us all? It was an amazing performance.'

'The Chilean Ambassador was there,' said Chris. 'You didn't see his face but I did.'

'I did see his face. What was the name of the girl – ?' said Hurley.

'Beatrice, Beatrice . . . Wademacher. No, Rademacher. She was that daughter, remember, of Rademacher.'

'That's right. It was some time in the 'seventies, mid-'seventies, when the Charismatic Revival was on. She said, "I think we should now pray and ask the Lord to bless us one by one." And she went on to name us all, didn't she?'

'No, only a few of us. She apparently didn't know all our names. But she laid her hands on every head, one by one.'

'Fundamentally', said Hurley, 'there was nothing wrong in acting as she did.'

'Don't you think so? If I remember, you didn't really like it any more than I did.'

'Not at the time, no, not at the time,' Hurley

said. 'But now, thinking back, in the abstract, there was an element of courage in that girl. I wonder what became of her.'

'I can't admire a religion that causes an upset and embarrasses people. There could be no objection to what she said, only the time and the place were wrong.'

'I quite agree.' Hurley laughed and then said, 'God, it was awful.'

'Wasn't it? Of course, there is that parable in the Bible about sending out to the highways and by-ways to make up a dinner party – there was a question of the host being at a loss because none of his guests could come. I wonder how it would work with us?'

'Going out in the street and stopping people: Come to dinner. One would probably be arrested.'

'Maybe a group of students would come,' mused Chris. 'Lower-middle-class students. They're more experimental and diversified than the upper classes.'

'I believe you're right,' said Hurley who had experience of students from the past. 'Maybe their table manners aren't of the finest, but somehow they inspire more affection, they make more fun.'

'To me,' said Chris, while the Sunday afternoon lazed on and the rain splashed at the windows, 'the lower classes always inspire more affection – looking back, it's the cooks and the greengrocers and the dressmakers that I remember with warmth, not the people I've met on social occasions. Bill was rich, of course, and a decent husband. I missed Bill when he died. But that was love, it really was. I'm talking about affection.'

'I know,' said Hurley. 'Our dinner to come: I feel a certain affection for everyone we've asked. Nearly everyone. I don't know Helen Suzy very well, and Margaret Damien hardly at all, and yet I can't get Margaret out of my head with her aggressive teeth and her honey-and-cream philosophy of *Les Autres.*'

'Perhaps you should paint her,' said Chris.

'I haven't done a portrait for years. I don't know if I could any more,' Hurley said, but he sounded reflective, so that Chris wondered if really he would like to sleep with Margaret. Chris thought of this without resentment. She herself had a minor attachment to a French orchestral conductor whom she saw nearly always when she went to Paris; she had a flat there and he stayed with her. But her real life was with Hurley and his with her.

'Hilda is convinced', she said, 'that William was in some way enticed into noticing Margaret in the first place.'

'Hilda has an exaggerated idea of her son's value, I should say,' said Hurley.

'Well, he's quite something on the marriage market. She has left everything, or almost everything, to William. He's the eldest son. It's in trust for him, and he gets it when Hilda dies. She thought that a good arrangement. She told me so herself. But you can't say he isn't a catch for a girl.'

'They'll have to wait a long time,' said Hurley. 'Hilda's flourishing. She'll live for ever.'

'Let's hope so. But she really is worried about her new daughter-in-law. It was so unlikely that they should just happen to meet in the fruit section of Marks & Spencer's. It actually could be a put-up job. She could have picked him up deliberately.'

'Look,' said Hurley, 'she spoke to him. He didn't need to answer at length, he didn't need to strike up an acquaintance. Do you realize that among the number of young people who get together these days very very few begin by being introduced?'

'Yes, I do know all that. Only Hilda is an old friend, Hurley. She told me that it was very spooky there in Fife at the wedding. Nothing you could put your finger on.'

'Oh, that's Scotland. All the families are odd, very odd.'

'Hilda said', Chris went on, 'that they weren't so odd. In fact they were too much all right.'

'She thinks they're after her money or her son's money. If I may say so,' said Hurley, 'you rich ladies always think in terms of money. The way you go on about it you'd think you were short of the stuff. You never stop talking about who's married who, and what the fortune is.'

Chris didn't refute this, although the accusation wasn't very true. She had plenty of other subjects to discuss, and generally did so. However, she said, 'It's a fascinating subject, Hurley, when you think, or half-think, just possibly a young man and his mother have been plotted against. You said yourself that you felt Margaret was strange.'

'Strange, yes,' he said, 'very strange.'

It was time for drinks. Their conversation became rather contrapuntal. He lamented the fact that he hadn't been near his studio the whole afternoon.

'It's Sunday,' she said, as if that were a factor of any sort.

He was vaguely looking at the mantelpiece. 'I adore the Salvation Army,' he said, with what relevance nobody will ever know.

'Nivea cream', Chris said presently, as she sipped her vodka and tonic, 'is my Proust's madeleine. The only reason I use it. Total recall.'

'Do you know,' mused Hurley, 'those champagne growers, the Ferrandi family, one of the cousins was killed by his wife with a blow on the head from a bottle of his own brand of champagne. The French make their bottles very heavy. Especially champagne.'

'Helen Suzy and Brian have accepted,' said Chris. 'I wonder how long that marriage will last?'

Luke, that Sunday afternoon, came round to see Chris about his employment as an extra at the forthcoming dinner party. To her surprise he brought her a flower, one single very long-stalked, very large-faced yellow dahlia.

'How nice of you, Luke,' she said, 'how really very delightful.' She was interviewing him in a comfortable sitting-room which was really a pantry attached to the kitchen. 'I believe you're an arts graduate?' she said.

'No, history, ma'am. I'm doing a post-graduate course at London University.'

'I do so admire you Americans the way you don't scorn manual work while you study.'

'I've always found my own education, ma'am. I work to eke out my grants. It's often a pleasure. And I believe I may benefit in the long run from the experiences I gain in so many different families, different homes.'

'We have a reference for you from Ernst Untzinger, a friend of Mr Reed's. It will be really good of you to come and help us out. I understand you're the perfect waiter, that'll be something to boast about when you get the Chair of History at an important university. Ernst refers to you as "Luke" by the way. How shall we call you?'

'Just Luke,' said Luke.

Chris was enchanted with his smile, his dark good looks, his easy manners. She thought, 'I'd far sooner have him as a guest at my table than hire him to wait on us.'

He told her, as is often the way with the young,

with their wide indiscriminate perspectives, how he aimed to go to China, when things had settled down, to South America, to North Africa, to Russia, maybe to study or to teach. Turkey, the Middle East. Not one after the other but all 'next summer'.

In came the chef from Mauritius, small, slim, Corby who was and looked about thirty, putting on his chef's cap and then tying his apron strings. When all these things were done he shook hands with Luke.

'Charterhouse is out at the moment. But he knows you're coming to help us serve.'

'That's right,' said Luke.

'I believe you know the Suzys,' said Corby with a slight accent of grandeur. 'Lord and Lady Suzy?'

'Only by hearsay,' said Luke.

'I'll leave you to talk,' said Chris. 'See you Thursday, 18th October.'

'What will you have?' said Corby. 'A beer? Cup of coffee?'

'Nothing, thanks. Charterhouse is the butler?'

'Well, yes, butler. You know a butler isn't really a butler unless he has a household of servants beneath him and a housekeeper to work with. It's like a general without an army. Here we don't even have a platoon. But Charterhouse has a butler's training. I was trained in Berne and Lyons.'

'I'd like to meet Charterhouse,' said Luke. 'Before the party.'

'Oh, just for a serving job it isn't necessary. I'll show you the dining-room. You've heard of the Suzys? They'll be here at the dinner.'

'You must get to know some interesting people,' said Luke. And he said, 'I've got to go now. Maybe I'll look in some time tomorrow, next day, and see Charterhouse. When's the best time?'

'Five o'clock,' said Corby. 'Five o'clock is always the best time for everybody and everything. You can't spend the best part of three years in Lyons without knowing it.'

'Ah,' said Luke. 'I'll remember that. I believe the Untzingers are coming to the dinner, do you know them at all?'

'By name,' said Corby. 'By name. Charterhouse would know them by sight. Another name that's on the list of guests is Damien. Multi-millionaires. Either husband and wife or mother and son, I couldn't tell you for sure.'

'Goodbye, Corby,' said Luke.

'Goodbye, Luke.'

Their goodbyes were not for long, for Luke did come round by the back door at five o'clock next day. He found Charterhouse in, and under cover of being shown the exact disposition of the serving table and sideboard of the dining-room – a veritable rehearsal – managed to obtain a great deal more information about the guests than he had obtained from Corby.

'People called Suzy,' said Charterhouse. 'A lord and a lady. Then people called – '

'I guess they did the Suzys',' said Luke.

'I daresay,' said Charterhouse. 'They were the people they burgled. They were actually upstairs asleep the whole time, they weren't out of London as supposed, but they got away with it, up to a point.' Luke did not seem puzzled by the identification of the alternative 'theys'. He obviously knew who Charterhouse meant. 'They', said Charterhouse, standing tall and dignified in Chris Donovan's blue dining-room, 'left a picture by early Francis Bacon on the wall and took a mirror instead. Utter fools. They only had the boot of a car and they said that's all they would fit in. When they found they'd been robbed they were gloating over the picture being left behind.'

Corby the chef appeared at the door of the dining-room.

'Chef?' said Charterhouse.

'Nothing,' said Corby.

'I am explaining to our young man,' said Charterhouse, 'the lay of the land for the forthcoming dinner.'

'It isn't no banquet,' said Corby.

'Banquet or no banquet,' said Charterhouse, 'to

me it is an occasion. I am a perfectionist as regards occasions.'

'I guess I'll manage,' said Luke.

'He should know who's who at the dinner,' said Charterhouse to Corby.

'Why?' said Corby. 'One serving one plate, is the same as any other plate. Unless there's a special diet present.'

'I'll manage, I guess,' said Luke who was decidedly nervous.

'If you guessed you'd manage why did you come back to see me?' said Charterhouse very cool, very lofty. 'Mr Corby, if you please.'

'What?' said Corby.

'Let me finish instructing our young man as to his duties and what they imply as regards the personalities expected.'

'Not necessary,' said Corby. Nevertheless, he retreated. Mrs Donovan and Mr Reed did rather appreciate Charterhouse, they respected his haughtiness. Those butler's manners were worth their weight in gold.

'Now,' said Charterhouse, when he was sure that the chef had gone right away out of earshot, 'another couple that will be here for the dinner and therefore away from home at that hour, are called Untzinger.'

'I know the Untzingers. Ella gets me jobs. She sent me here.'

'Their surroundings?'

'Comfortable. But nothing much for our friends. We should be careful.'

'A Mr Roland Sykes. Unmarried. He has money. His things should be of interest. There is a couple newly married called Damien. Now, you ask your executive people about the Damiens. His mother is a multi-millionaire. I'm not sure, but I imagine she'll be at the dinner. If she's of any interest, and she should be of interest, let me know. I'll write out a list of addresses for you.'

Luke's role was merely that of informer. He had started off as a genuine party-helper, employed by catering firms and private people. And he was, indeed, a genuine post-graduate in modern history. Some months ago he had been approached by a fellow-waiter at a grand and luxurious wedding. 'I wish', said the waiter, 'I had a list of these guests and their addresses. All absent from home hours and hours today. A list would be worth a fortune.'

Luke was puzzled at first, but remarkably quick to perceive the point. He loaded his tray with champagne and orange juice, ready to circulate with it outside the marquee. He looked at his fellow-labourer and cast a glance round the hundreds of guests. 'The moneyed class,' murmured Luke. 'That's right,' said his companion behind the white cloth-covered table. He was there to serve special requests. 'Whisky and soda, sir? Of course. Which brand?'

At the end of that long Saturday of the country wedding, Luke went back up to London by car with his new friend who asked to be called Garnet. They went to a club to eat and relax. And there Luke learned of the exact prices to be gained by anyone with a list of good names, or even one name, present at a party and therefore away from home. Luke and Garnet, who also boasted a few more reliable members of his team, were assured of their pay whether the names were useful or not, as Garnet pointed out. 'More often than not', confided Garnet, 'it's too risky. Servants, guards, in the house. Dogs. Sophisticated alarms. They're alarms that go off at the police station but not in the house, so the police have time to come and catch the fools. All that is no concern of us. Sometimes the people don't go to the dinner or whatever at the last minute. Not our fault. No concern of us. We give the list and take the money. It could be done by word of mouth, no proof. As I say, a list like the wedding today would be worth a lot. Somebody else no doubt provided one. But, as I say, even if it's a duplicate a list is a list and the principals pay. They like to encourage. They're generous, as I say.'

As Garnet said they would be, they had been generous with Luke. He had been far enough away from any field of action not to feel any guilt. Ella and Ernst would have said they could trust Luke with their lives. They wouldn't ever need to lock anything up with Luke in the house. They were right. They had no idea how greatly Luke prospered.

'Luke, I have a friend, the artist Hurley Reed and his life-companion, extremely charming Chris Donovan. They're giving a party. We'll be there. Will you give them an evening of your time to help with the serving?'

'I think so,' said Luke. 'Hopefully I'll be free.' To Ella this meant he would certainly take on the job. She had never known him refuse.

It was only the matter of the very expensive watch that gave them to think, and then they thought wrongly, both arriving at the immediate conclusion that Luke had received this many-thousand-dollar treasure in return for sexual favours.

Helen Suzy was writing to her friend, Brian Suzy's daughter.

Dear Pearl,

I suppose Brian wrote and told you about our robbery. You can imagine he was very upset, in fact a bit too upset in my humble opinion. I know you warned me he's another generation, they think of their goods and chattels. You can't take it with you. Pearl, I think sometimes I'm going crazy. He says he's been raped, how would he know about rape? In fact in a funny psychological way he wants to be raped, they say we all do!!! I feel I sympathize with your Mother when she was married to him. But it's still another generation. I was truly sorry our stuff was stolen, and that they urinated all over. We had to get the walls done anyway. I never liked those chair covers. Now we hear the gang is operating outside London, a house in Dulwich and a big house in Wembley. The people were out but they wounded a servant who is still in hospital. The police say it's the same gang as came to us. They seem to know. We were in bed. We could have been killed. They seem to have found out in the other cases when people were out to dinner or the theatre. The big thing as Brian will have told you was they left the Picture on the wall by Francis Bacon, very costly. Now he's cutting down on the phone etc. to make up for our losses, so I didn't ring you up. In my humble opinion we should spend more to cheer ourselves up like a trip to Venice. Brian says maybe yes, a trip to Venice, so I put an idea in his head perhaps. We have a couple of dinner parties then we could go off. He has a burglar alarm put in the corner of the rooms that blinks electronically, but not in the bedroom. I put my foot down at that. You can imagine!

What happened about that boy, the one you met at the Poetry reading at the Y? Did he leave for London? He hasn't shown up. You couldn't come before Christmas I suppose? There can't be much on at the UN, so much is happening this end. Get me one jar Rennett's Formula Twenty-three from Saks if it is still going. Charge it on card. I wish you could come soon. Beatrice, the first Lady Suzy before your Mother's turn rang up very officiously about the robbery when she read of it in the papers, telling me what to do. All the china and so on was really hers. I said it was a bit late in the day to say all this, she'd better write to Brian or his solicitor. She can drop dead, with his china and her glassware. I didn't tell Brian she rang. Why upset him more?

Tons of love. Do write.

Helen

9

THE little through-street off the Gray's Inn Road, in the area of St Pancras in London, was not very active at two in the afternoon. A three-storey nineteenth-century house was the modest Anglican convent of Mary of Good Hope. The street, only a few yards long, and narrow, was closed to traffic. Its usual pedestrians were lawyers and office workers taking a short cut. Margaret Murchie, however, arrived on her motor-bike, parked on the pavement and pressed the bell. She had an appointment to be interviewed as a novice. A minister of an Episcopalian church in Scotland had made this arrangement.

It was shortly after the death by murder of her grandmother at the Calton Nursing Home in Edinburgh that Margaret had gone into a silence; she was also thinner and paler. The public fuss had died down, Margaret's aunts had made off with their loot, and her father had made himself comfortable with his mother's fortune. But nothing would induce Margaret to benefit from the money. She made this well known. Her family and their friends were impressed by her attitude. Her sad pallor and silence were deeply felt, too, by Margaret's fellow-workers in the ceramics studio in Glasgow. It came about, now, that everyone was sorry for Margaret. Even her sisters, in their different ways, expressed pity for her suffering and the wrong that everyone had done her in their secret thoughts. Only Dan Murchie, passionate and bemused by his daughter, could not prevent himself from half-wondering what she was up to, without fully realizing that he was wondering at all.

'I always said,' wrote Flora to her mother, 'that one thing had nothing to do with another. And now you can see that Margaret had nothing to do with the unfortunate incident. Must close now as it's bed time and I have to run my bath.' Eunice wrote: 'It was a great relief to Peter and I that nothing came of the scandal after all. It would have been so bad for me in my condition. Poor Margaret was questioned much too long by the police and too often. And now as you say she looks ill. I'm not surprised. It was hard enough on Peter and I.'

Margaret's ring at the bell brought a nun to the door, a young woman in a pale grey dress of a modern length and with a grey and white veil on her head.

'I have an appointment,' said Margaret, 'with Sister Lorne.'

'She's expecting you. If that's your bike would you mind bringing it into the courtyard? Just a minute and I'll get the key.'

She shut the front door again completely, but after a few moments appeared again with a large key with which she opened a side-door. Margaret wheeled her motor-cycle into the courtyard which was bare except for a six-passenger panel van. 'You can come up this way, Miss Murphy,' said the girl.

'Murchie,' said Margaret.

'Oh, sorry, I heard "Murphy". This way.'

Beeswax was the smell Margaret had always heard that convents smelled of. She saw that the wooden banisters and the stairs were brightly polished and felt that the rather musky fragrance in the air must be beeswax. In fact it was an aerosol spray but that did not detract from the austere clean conventual atmosphere of the house. Plain cord matting formed the stair carpet. Margaret was shown in to a small sitting-room with elephant-grey plastic-seated chairs, a round table with a lace centrepiece on which stood a vase of coloured glass flowers and a desk on which were piled some brown cardboard folders containing ragged papers, a four-part London telephone directory and a black telephone. There were plain nylon curtains in the two windows, which had long curtains at each side made of some homespun green and brown stuff.

Margaret draped herself as far as that was possible on one of the chairs, her head to one side with an arm resting on the chair-back. In came a middle-aged woman dressed in her short grey habit and floating veil. She breathed heavily as if with a chest complaint. 'Miss Murchie?' she said. 'I'm Sister Lorne, the deputy Superior. Our Reverend Mother is in bed, not well at all. We all have to look after her.' She paused for breath, put her hand to her chest. 'To tell you the truth,' she said, 'I smoke too much.'

'Is that allowed in a convent?' Margaret said.

'Oh, goodness, yes. We're a very modern order, you know. Few people realize how the C of E has marched on. They think the old-fashioned dogmas still prevail; they think the repressive colonial missionary system of the upper classes can bring our message of Good Hope to the Third World. Have they read Marx? – No. Would they under-stand – under – stand with a hyphen – his message to the toiling masses? – No. We of the Order of Good Hope – '

'Can I help you? – A glass of water?' said Margaret springing up from her chair, since the emphysemic nun at this point had broken down into a distressing condition of wheeze and puff. Sister Lorne waved Margaret's offer away while she clung to the edge of the table, recovering.

She recovered eventually. 'Thank you,' she said to Margaret. 'It shows a good spirit to make a gesture of help. I had a letter from the Reverend Mr Wise and of course he explained your case. I read it to our sisters after prayers last night. There are only nine of us including our sick Superior. We all agreed to pray that you would suit us as a novice. There are few real vocations in these days of yuppies and murky capitalism. I hope you have one. You were *sent*. I can only say you were sent.'

'I feel sent,' said Margaret. 'It is a most extraordinary feeling.'

It is sad to observe that of those nine nuns of St Pancras only three were of vital interest, and that those three were fairly unprincipled. The remaining six were devout and dutiful, and two of them very sweet and trusting, but all those six were as dreary as hell.

Margaret made great progress as a novice at the Convent of Good Hope. Their mission was largely in social work, and as they had a small community and limited funds, this was mainly confined to hospital visiting. The liturgy of the morning consisted of a psalm and prayers. They busied themselves about the housekeeping, the shopping and the cooking all morning. After lunch, which was very simple and served with hot water to drink, they set forth on their visits to elderly patients who had no friends or relatives to visit them.

Margaret made herself useful as a frugal shopper. On her motor-bike she would go to buy their daily rations at Clerkenwell and Finsbury where the food shops were cheaper and the wares not much inferior.

Dear Dad,

It is quite a good life, and I believe I have a vocation. It is all a question of thinking of *les autres*. Of course, yes, you can come and visit. But not just yet.

Sister Lorne is standing in for the Mother Superior. She is a leftie, as you would call it, but that's the result of thinking of *les autres*. The old men and the old women in those hospital wards would make you left wing if you could see them.

Sister Marrow has a big say in running the convent. She's the Novice Mistress. She has a wild artistic temperament, sometimes breaking the glasses set out on the table in the refectory. We get hot water to drink, a drop of sherry on Sunday with the vicar after the service. Well, to get back to Sister Marrow she is known as the four-letter nun. She makes Sister Lorne laugh and I see why. Sister Rooke is a master plumber, you wouldn't believe how much in demand. She was sent for by the Bishop as he couldn't get a plumber in the whole of London, at least not one who understood those antique drains. The other nuns I'm afraid are lacking in a bit of IQ, at least so it seems to me. But they go forth with their little basket of goodies over their arm like little Red Riding Hood to visit the sick, except of course their capes are grey like we all wear. Sister Rooke doesn't use four-letter words, she says you're more of a plumber if you use the words that stretch to five, six, seven letters.

Sister Lorne is furious because the Bishop sent a dictionary to Sister Marrow. He said he had been given to understand she was at a loss for words, how to express herself. He wrote something like that. And he recommended she should study the dictionary or look it up when the accurate epithet was called for. We had a meeting about the letter. Sister Lorne has written back to the Bishop that this was an insult. She said that four-letter words were the lifeblood of the market place, the People's parlance and aphrodisiac, the dynamic and inalienable prerogative of the proletariat. Sister Marrow added a PS. Fuck your balls Bishop, you are a fart and a shit. I posted the letter myself. The Bishop can't do a thing. Sister Lorne remarked that there is no power in Church or State that can stop the inexorable march of Marxism into the future.

The old Mother Superior is in bed. Such a tragic case.

Kisses to Mum and all.

Margaret

This letter was shown to Magnus the next Sunday, after lunch. He was tweedily dressed, with a deerstalker hat which he kept on in the house in case of cold. 'Conceivably', said Magnus, 'what she says is true. But some of it may be the fruit of a fertile Scottish imagination. The Murchies of old were great cursers, oath-takers and foul-mouthers; it was known of them on both sides of the Border. I could cite the manuscript sources.'

'I never thought of her account not being genuine,' said Dan. 'Greta and I just felt she had got in with a funny lot.'

'Undoubtedly. But as she is still under shock, she probably sees things double, treble, not as they really are.'

'Of course this nun-business won't last,' said Dan. 'She'll be out before long. At the same time, as a picture of what the churches are producing her letter doesn't seem too exaggerated. A friend of mine in Suffolk – the vicar wears one ear-ring and his boy-friend serves at the altar in a dazzling gold cope lined with black satin. The Bishops can't do a thing about it, and half the time they're just as bad.'

'I don't like the sound of the old Mother Superior lying sick in the attic,' said Magnus.

'Attic?' said Dan, lifting the letter to scrutinize it. 'She doesn't say attic.'

'It sounds like an attic,' said Magnus. 'I hope nothing is going to happen to the old lady.'

'Oh, God!' said Dan. 'Oh, God!'

'Hot water to drink on week-days and a drop of sherry on Sunday,' Magnus remarked as Greta came in with whisky, water and two glasses on a tray. 'One for the road, Magnus,' said Greta.

'I just showed Magnus the letter I got from Margaret,' said Dan. He poured neat whisky for Magnus and one for himself with water. 'Don't overdo it,' Greta said.

'Magnus has just raised the question whether what Margaret says is true or not,' said Dan.

'Oh, I daresay it's true,' said Greta. 'We have a friend in Suffolk – you have no idea the carry-on. The vicar wears an ear-ring and – '

'Dan just told me,' said Magnus. 'All I say is, true or not is neither here nor there. The fact is we don't know a thing about what Margaret does with her life at night. I don't, myself, see Margaret getting into bed by ten.'

'She is very sincere about this venture,' Greta said.

'Sincerity is neither here nor there. The fact remains that madness commonly takes the form of religious mania,' said Magnus, not in the least troubled by any thought that this might apply to himself. 'In fact,' he said, 'Margaret is a Murchie, Covenanting stock who refused to accept the rule of bishops. It is written in the scriptures, Samuel 9: 11, "According to all that my lord the king hath commanded his servant, so shall thy servant do."

Which you should meditate: Margaret might well be under divine orders. And again it is written, Proverbs 26: 17, "He that passeth by, and meddleth with strife belonging not to him, is like one that taketh a dog by the ears." You can work that one out for yourselves.' Magnus swigged down his whisky and reached for more.

'No more, Magnus, it's bad for you,' said Greta. She looked very wild-eyed.

'Time to go home, Magnus,' said Dan, standing up. Magnus heaved himself up, chuckling to himself. He followed Dan, but turned at the sitting-room door and said to Greta, 'Do you know anything of hypnotism? It's at the bottom of witchcraft, you know. Remember Orpheus with his lute.'

'Come on, Magnus,' said Dan.

'Yes, goodbye, Magnus,' said Greta.

Shortly after Margaret's arrival at the convent the BBC television came to do a profile of the Sisters of Good Hope. The preliminary arrangements had been made some months before between the Mother Superior and the director of the programme, a young woman with long yellow hair and hard blue eyes who wore dark skirts to her ankles and heavy boots. The short-skirted Mother Superior, then in fairly good health, had shown her over the premises and given a rational account of what the Sisters did with their time. Rita Jones, the young director, was introduced to the nine-nun community. She made copious notes in her desk-size filofax. 'Of course, Miss Jones,' said the Mother Superior, 'we are not all cut to measure like the more ancient monastic orders. We are extremely individualistic in our tastes, in our personalities, in our backgrounds, in our views on life and society, including religion and politics.' Miss Jones took note of this on a blue page of her filofax.

'There has been talk that your community might be leaving the Church of England. Is that likely to happen?'

'Oh, it could happen, but not for a good while,' said Sister Lorne, perceiving that the question was, basically, whether it was worth planning a programme if in fact the community was in a state of flux.

'Sister Marrow – she's our Novice Mistress, except we have no novices at present – has not yet finished painting her masterpiece, a mural in our refectory. It will take time, months, years. Sister Marrow is an artist.'

'Can I see the painting?'

'Oh, not yet. I'll have to ask Sister Marrow. But we can promise to have something ready to televise if you decide to come.' Sister Lorne lowered her voice. 'Sister Marrow has temperament. Naturally. But she's very sound basically. Very with it, very *politicized* like myself.' She raised her voice again and pronounced, 'Religion pure and simple is not enough.'

'About the hospital visiting,' said Miss Jones. 'That is your main concern, isn't it?'

'Yes, it's our mission,' said Sister Lorne. 'We do just that. Whatever criticism may be levelled at us, nobody can say that we don't visit the sick. It's a very important work. We are widely appreciated.'

'Yes, I know. That's why we thought of a profile.' Rita Jones evidently smelt a possible good programme in that phrase 'whatever criticism . . .' She asked, 'Can you say something about the criticism?'

'No,' said Sister Lorne.

Miss Jones changed tack: 'Would it be possible for us to take some shots of the members of your community visiting the sick in hospital?' And on hearing that the Sisters of Good Hope would have no objection, the programme had been agreed upon.

Before she left Miss Jones said, 'Take care of your chest, Sister Lorne. It sounds like bronchitis.'

So it happened that shortly after Margaret Murchie had joined the community as a novice the BBC duly arrived: Miss Jones, a team of five and their cameras. The first thing they did was to change the lighting arrangements in the recreation room and the refectory, clobbering through the hall with their unnecessarily stout boots. Sister Marrow appeared in the hallway. 'What the fucking hell do you think you're doing?' she enquired of the chief cameraman, who was immediately joined protectively by the other four technicians.

'Are you a nurse, then?' asked one of the men.

'No, I'm a Novice Mistress. Now, what are you doing with this trail of crap?' She indicated the photographic gear and a long trail of wiring leading out from the refectory. Just then Margaret appeared through the front door. 'Sister Murchie, our new novice,' said Sister Marrow. 'Meet the team,' she said to Margaret. 'They think they're going to film the fucking refectory but they've no bloody right. My work, my unfinished painting is there. Not ready for the crapulous public to take in.'

A voice from the landing above said, 'Sister Marrow, I *did* promise . . .' It was Sister Lorne leaning over the banisters. Miss Jones was with her. 'The refectory is an essential,' she said. The bemused camera team looked up towards Miss Jones for further orders.

'Follow me,' said Margaret. 'I'll explain the painting to you. It is by far the most important thing in the convent. Sister Marrow is much too modest.'

'Shit,' said Sister Marrow.

Sister Lorne and Miss Jones came tripping down the stairs to join the bewildered crew and Margaret in the refectory. Sister Marrow, tall and skinny, followed behind. 'She hasn't been here three weeks and she fucking well runs the convent,' was Sister Marrow's comment on young Sister Murchie. But she seemed pleased that Margaret was about to draw attention to her mural.

It was so far only a sketch, stretching along one side of the refectory wall. It depicted a long, huge, antiquated monster, blowing clouds of smoke. 'Is that a dragon?' said Miss Jones, avid for symbolism.

'No it's the sketch of a train. A steam train,' said Sister Lorne loud and clear.

'Oh, a train,' said Miss Jones. 'Would that be Freudian?'

'Freudian my arse,' said Sister Marrow in a booming voice from the doorway.

'Are those saints?' said one of the camera crew, a slight and sensitive-looking youth.

'Saints? What do you mean?' said Sister Lorne. The vaguely painted-in figures standing beside the train did indeed have some sort of halo or bushy cloud around their heads. One particular figure seemed to have descended from the train, his halo bigger and bushier than the rest, with one arm raised, his finger pointing upwards.

'As I am given to understand it,' said Margaret in a quiet civilized tone of voice that implied a lack of civilized perception in all the others present, 'this mural painting is a depiction of the scene at the railway station in St Petersburg on 16 April

1917, when Vladimir Ilich Ulyanov known as Lenin arrived from Switzerland to be met by a great crowd of comrades.'

'You give them haloes, then?' said Miss Jones.

'Those are fur hats, you silly cow,' muttered Sister Marrow.

'I don't quite get the religious significance,' said Miss Jones. ' – Oh, well, yes. I do. I think I do. That half-naked figure with the beard and the loincloth lying along the cloud of steam and leaning his torso over the cloud to touch Lenin must be God.' The figure she referred to was up near the refectory's ceiling. Lenin was looking up at it with his raised arm, so that his finger touched the pointing finger of the bearded man.

'Not God. Karl Marx,' said Sister Lorne, wheezing heavily. 'You must get your points of reference right.' She looked hard at a member of the BBC who had reflectively lit a cigarette. 'No smoking,' she said.

One of the cameramen moved to set up his tripod in the doorway where Sister Marrow was standing. She blocked his way. 'Watch your balls, Sister,' he said.

'You like pushing women around, don't you?' said Sister Marrow.

'Yes, I do.'

Five days of filming and interviewing ensued, including a round of visits to the hospitals where many of the staff and patients put up a resistance to the intrusion. Margaret, being extremely photogenic, was induced to be photographed administering to the more grateful of the patients; she arranged their pillows and the flowers on the ward tables. But it was inside the convent that the team got their supreme moments. Rita Jones was delighted. The eventual public were divided into two parts as they always are when religious questions arise, and this ensured the success of the programme. It was repeated two weeks after its first showing, in spite of the protests of the protesting half of the public. Only Sister Marrow's speeches were modified, although not quite. Sister Rooke, a round-faced girl with warts and a cheery smile, large but compact, wearing her veil but with a plumber's overalls, explained in her television-worthy North Country accent how she had come to be a master plumber; and she described the various ecclesiastical places whose complicated drainage systems she had to plumb. In reply to Miss Jones's questions she recounted her experiences at the installation of washing machines, dishwashers, central-heating arrangements, bathrooms and showers. About Sister Rooke, at least, the total television audience was unanimous. Everyone loved Sister Rooke and also the plumber's mate, a certain Sister Rose, very young, equally veiled and overalled.

Sister Lorne's statement in the course of an interview was perhaps the most impressive to one part of the public and offensive to the outraged other: 'The march of Marxist philosophy and politics etcetera will not stop at the borders. Our young will pour into the Eastern European countries pleading asylum from the capitalist-consumer system. We will live to see the day.' The outraged part of the public were not in the least concerned with the probability or otherwise of Sister Lorne's prophecy coming true; they were indignant only that a nun of the Church of England had said it.

The convent had returned to its routine after the incursion of the television crew. Sister Marrow applied herself to her refectory mural. After the programme was released, she seethed with aggrieved rage against the *Observer* television critic who had understood her mural to depict 'Anna Karenina at the railway station'. She was somewhat placated by an apology and a corrected description of her masterpiece, which the newspaper printed in a spare corner.

In the course of the five-day filming of the programme the ailing Mother Superior rallied and was able to be brought down to her winged arm-chair in the recreation room. She declared herself to feel perfectly all right except that she couldn't endure to be left alone and she couldn't sleep with the light off. So long as she had some company, she assured Miss Jones, who interviewed her, and so long as she didn't have to sleep in the dark she could be counted as an active vigorous Nun of Good Hope. 'The others thought I was going to die. They look at me as if I was a ghost, or my face a skull and my body a skeleton under my habit.'

'Surely not,' said Miss Jones.

'Surely yes,' said the aged woman, sitting upright enough in her wing chair. 'Especially Sister Lorne: who milked the cow with the crumpled horn. Do you know who the cow is? – Everything is symbolic. I'll tell you who the cow is. Sister Lorne's husband. She married a farm-boy with clammy hands and huge big round eyes. He looks at you like a cow. Sister Lorne is the maiden all forlorn who milked – or maybe it's tossed – the cow with the crumpled horn.'

Miss Jones registered all this but later edited it out, so that it never appeared in the programme. In fact, none of the Mother Superior's speeches was reproduced, and she looked absolutely sublime sitting there with her visible charm to grace the programme. However, Rita Jones, the clever girl, thought she might as well ask Sister Lorne if it was true she had once been married. 'I am married,' said Sister Lorne.

'Married? Isn't that against your vows?'

'Yes,' said Sister Lorne. 'But he worked on a farm. Ecology comes before vows.'

'Oh yes, but I don't quite follow,' said Miss

Jones. 'Your Mother Superior was quoting from "The House that Jack Built".'

'Really? What did she say?'

'That you were married to a young farmer, Sister Lorne.'

'The farmer sowing his corn, who married the maiden all forlorn . . . Is that what she said?'

'Something like that. Of course I'm not going to use it in the programme. Your Mother Superior obviously wanders in her mind. But I just – '

'You're right, you're not going to use it in the programme. She thinks I want to step into her shoes.'

'I just wondered if your husband ever comes to the convent?'

'Now and again.'

'May I say just that?'

'No, no. As a matter of fact it would be impossible to prove. The other nuns wouldn't like it. He comes dressed as a curate,' she confided. Sister Lorne smiled, breathing heavily.

Miss Jones had already got plenty of unusual material, so she thought it wise to drop this alarming and rather cloudy subject.

But Margaret, whose job it had become to keep the old nun company, and who occupied another bed in the same bedroom, had plenty of opportunity to hear variations on the theme of Sister Lorne and her imputed spouse. Margaret kept an eye open for a curate with large round eyes.

Two months after the successful transmission of the BBC programme Sister Rose, the much-loved and admirable young plumber's assistant, was found dead in the little convent courtyard. She had been strangled but not raped or sexually assaulted in any way. The girl was large and strong; she had been strangled by a pair of large hands. It was not established whether her killer was a man or a woman.

Big and manly as were some of the nuns of Good Hope, it happened that not one of them possessed excessively large hands. This did not entirely exclude some nun in a *raptus* of homicidal strength from having committed the crime, but it weakened the possibility. The male frequenters of the convent, two priests and the agricultural husband of Sister Lorne, were also excluded, the priests because one was in Fulham at the time of the murder and the other was on a plane to Glasgow. Sister Lorne's spouse was at the time in a boarding-house at Cirencester where she had sent him to study agriculture at the college there, and make a man of him.

The nuns were now being questioned closely, interrogated one by one. So far, nobody knew, had seen, heard or suspected anything. It had not even reached Margaret's turn when the Mother Superior wove her way into the refectory where a man from Scotland Yard was taking notes from Sister Rooke;

the old lady leaned against the much-adorned wall and confessed to the murder.

This was unlikely though not impossible. Her confession was taken note of in the greatest detail and put aside by the police, as it were for a rainy day. The interrogations of the nuns continued while the Mother Superior was ushered up to bed. There she suffered cardiac arrest, rallied, confirmed her confession, asked for and received the Last Sacrament, and died. According to her statement the Reverend Mother was indignant about a remark Sister Rose had made in the course of the late television programme. She had told her interviewer that she wasn't quite content in the convent. 'What about the life of the spirit?' she said. 'Why don't we have a spiritual life?' She had gone on to complain that the nunnery was virtually nothing but an entity in the National Health Service and that the Mother Superior was the top culprit in this situation.

Most of the nuns had a firm alibi for the hour of the crime, and those who had not had no motive. Margaret, who was interrogated with the others, had been on a visit to her sister Eunice in Dulwich that night, 'to see her new nephew'.

The Mother Superior's hands had not been noticeably large. A re-run of the discarded sequences of the television programme, which had cut out her speeches, was made for the benefit of the police. They studied the whole film with predatory attention. The Mother Superior's confession did seem to alter radically her image as she sat lording it in the wing chair. So long as she didn't have to sleep in the dark, she had told Miss Jones, she was to be counted on as an active and vigorous member of the community. Her voice seemed to linger on, and emphasize, the words 'active' and 'vigorous'. Even the toughest of the detective inspectors felt a slight shiver as she went on: 'The others thought I was going to die (slight accent on 'I'). They look at me as if I was a ghost, or my face a skull and my body a skeleton under my habit.'

'It's her, all right,' said one of the policemen. By the time they came to the interview with the murdered girl ('. . . this convent is nothing more than an entity in the National Health Service. Where is the spiritual side of life? . . .') they were all disposed to fall back on the evident solution: the Mother Superior's confession. It was too late to interrogate her further.

The trouble was, none of the investigators sincerely believed she had committed the murder, even though by a stretch of logic she could have done it. They were looking at least for an accomplice. In her room was found a handbook on karate, which all the other members of the community professed to have never seen before.

The television news re-ran portions of the original programme, accompanied by Sister Lorne's comments. 'This is the end of the community of Good Hope,' she said. 'Most of the younger nuns have left. We can't help feeling the hand of the supernatural in this tragic event. The house is to be taken over by a firm of lawyers.'

Margaret wrote:

Dear Dad,

I'll be home again on Saturday. For good.

It is terrible to be within touching distance of a murder so soon after the last. Fortunately as you heard the Mother Superior's confession relaxed the atmosphere. The police here were extremely polite to us all, and in my case there was no repetition of all that grilling I underwent on poor Granny's death. Nobody can understand how the Mother Superior could have been physically, let alone morally, capable of such an action. There is something mysterious. It seems the Mother Superior was practising karate. How could she do that in her condition?

I can't help feeling it all has to do with that television programme. One of the crew left a letter on my pillow asking for a date. Of course that proves nothing. Just his cheek.

I got a letter from Uncle Magnus. He knows I was with Eunice at the time. But he hints, he throws his suspicions on me without any evidence at all. Do you know he even quoted

Schopenhauer at me anent my alibi – 'Chronology is not causality.' Poor old fellow. I could sue him for that.

This place has been sold. Nearly everyone's left. There are three nuns still doing their hydrotherapy (washing-up) in the kitchen and Sister Lorne acting general manager. Sister Marrow is going to be an art teacher at a girls' school and Sister Rooke is going to continue with her plumbing when her nerves permit. Very few think of les autres.

Love to Mum.

Margaret

10

S HORTLY after the wedding of Margaret and William Damien, Hilda Damien telephoned twice from Australia to Chris Donovan. The second time she asked Chris if she or Hurley would supervise and keep a check on a purchase she had arranged through a sale at Sotheby's of a painting by Monet.

Hurley had come in from his studio, his day's work over, when he heard of this request. He was more than willing to be involved in this interesting deal; he was positively excited. Hilda, so Chris told him, had instructed her lawyer in London to give Hurley Reed free access to the deal and to decide about the safekeeping of the picture.

Charterhouse passed a tray with Chris's dry martini, the latter with the glass expertly iced. He was always ready with the drinks at this hour. He busied himself with Hurley's whisky and soda with ice.

'What Monet is it?' said Hurley.

'She didn't say. You know what Hilda's like. She just buys "a Monet".'

Hurley gave a smile between tolerance and scorn. But he said, 'I'll soon find out. Does she intend to take it to Australia?'

'No. Do you know what? In spite of all she said, she's weakened and decided to give it to the young couple as an additional wedding present. But it's to be a secret. She's going to take it in to their flat in Hampstead and give them a surprise.'

'I thought she'd given them the actual flat?'

'Yes, well now they're getting the Monet as well.'

'What did she pay for it?'

'I don't know,' said Chris. She sipped her welcome dry martini.

'I'll find out. I expect it was a lot. Too much.'

Charterhouse had left the room.

Luke in the public phone box said:

'I just dialogued with the butler.'

'And?'

'It's confirmed for October 18th.'

'And?'

'People called Suzy, a titled man and a titled woman.'

'We've done the Suzys. A waste of time.'

'Untzingers. They're friends of mine, though. Not rich, I mean like the rich are rich.'

'What name?'

'Untzinger. I'd be obliged if – '

'I'd be obliged if you'd continue.'

'Damien.'

'Damien!'

'Yes, Damien. Mother and son he seemed to think are expected. She's been doing up a flat in Hampstead. A picture on the wall by that artist named Monet, that French – '

'You said Monet?'

'Just bought it, just the other day.'

It was ten days before Chris Donovan's dinner party.

There was 'flu in the air and Roland Sykes had caught it. He sat up in a chair in the sitting-room of his flat. Annabel had come round to look after him. 'You should go to bed,' she said.

He was fiddling with a bundle of press cuttings.

'That person Murchie who is going to be at Chris Donovan's dinner,' he said. 'I've remembered. I worked on some archives for the solicitor who represented two of her aunts. They were contesting a will. It was settled out of court. But look at the background – I knew there was something sensational. The grandmother of the Margaret Murchie who married the Damien boy was murdered.'

He sipped his hot whisky and water while Annabel read the press cutting with avid attention.

'It doesn't do your 'flu any good but it makes you feel better,' Roland said, meaning his drink.

'My God! I've seen that face before,' Annabel suddenly said. She had a newspaper article with a large picture of Margaret, sub-titled 'Margaret Murchie – questioned by the police'.

'It was all over the papers at the time,' Roland said.

'No, but I've seen it since. Somewhere on the television. Within the past year. Nothing to do with the Murchie murder. It was some kind of popular programme, cultural programme . . . I don't know. I'd have to think, find out.'

'I wonder', said Roland 'if Hurley and Chris know about the Murchie murder story.'

'Why? Do you think of drawing their attention to it?'

'Well, it might be interesting.'

'If I were in your place,' she said, 'I would keep it to myself. It would only make you out to be bitchy. You don't want the name of being bitchy, do you?'

'I don't know,' said Roland, drawing his woollen dressing-gown tight round his neck. 'Whisky can't be a remedy, you know. It only makes you feel better.'

'I'll make you another,' said Annabel. 'You shouldn't ring up Hurley and Chris to tell them something denigratory about one of their forth-coming guests. It's crude.'

'Maybe,' said Roland, putting his hand to his head to signify how much the 'flu was upon him.

When Annabel came back from the kitchen with another glass of hot whisky she said, 'I wish I could remember what programme that girl Murchie was on. It was something unusual.'

Helen wrote:

Dear Pearl,

Your letter made me laugh so much. I hope you have a good time at the ball. Brian says he doesn't mind the postponement of your trip so long as you're having a good time. I went to the fashion show at the Metropole in Brighton, a lot of nothing new. Those starving girls, but still the men like it when you look like some kind of Barbie doll.

Do you think I have the Stockholm syndrome? You know what that is. It's when you're so grateful to the man that's holding you prisoner just because he treats you better sometimes than the other times or than other people. Then you actually take an affection for the one that knocks you about the least. I don't say Brian knocks me about in the real sense, but he goes on about the robbery. Why else I should stay with your dear father I really do not know.

He has gone off today thank God to the House of Lords to express his demented opinions about things that go towards the rule and government of us his perfectly sane fellow citizens. Then home again tonight and believe me it will be the robbery again for dinner. After all they left the Francis Bacon on the wall. Do you know what the next move is? The picture is to go in the bank. I won't miss the picture but it's just the idea of putting paintings in the bank. Sometimes I feel the age gap is just too wide and sometimes I don't.

We're going to dinner with that fun painter Hurley Reed. You remember you liked them so much and his wife, I suppose one should say friend, Chris. After that a trip to Venice, how lovely, I can't wait.

Encl. is a cheque for you. I had him write it out before he left for the Lords while he was in the mood. Cash it quick before he puts the money in a vault.

All love,
　　Helen

Ella and Ernst were in the drivers' lounge of the cross-Channel ferry on the way home from Brussels. It was the second day of his having his beard removed, and he kept on putting his hand to his chin, stroking the beard that was.

'I hope', she said, 'that Luke remembered to turn on the heating.'

'We can turn it on and go out to eat.'

'It isn't easy, going out to eat, after Brussels,' said Ella, who liked her food.

Ernst was busy with papers in the briefcase open on his knee. 'Luke,' he said.

'What about Luke?'

'He might be there, waiting for us.' He smiled at her, frankly acknowledging that she would regard this as a sort of treat.

'Why, did you ring him up?' she said.

'Yes, I did.'

'Well, we can take him out to dinner with us.'

Ernst touched his non-existent beard. 'Yes, we can. That's what I thought.'

Ella went to stretch her legs in the dilapidated ferry which chugged its way to Dover. The windows were coated with oily grey dirt, the painted frames were chipped. She walked the length of the boat among passengers dressed unsuitably for the season, in bright holiday colours, as they always did in the fanciful belief that across the Channel lay summertime. Ella nosed round the duty-free gift shop and came back.

'I could have bought him a Waterman pen,' she said.

Ernst smiled. 'With his looks he can get more than a Waterman pen,' he said.

Luke was the main thing they now had in common. It had positively begun to draw them together, so that they were actually further from separating than they had ever been in their married life.

'That watch,' said Ella. 'You know there are fakes, copies. There is a big trade in copies of prestigious goods.'

'It might be a fake,' said Ernst, 'but knowing Luke I don't see why it should be.'

'I hope he's all right,' said Ella. 'That's all, I hope he's all right and takes care of himself.'

'That's what I hope. There's something very appealing about his willingness to take these serving and catering jobs. It shows a decent side.'

'He called me', said Ella, 'about a couple of likely flats he'd seen, suitable for us. In Bloomsbury. What do you think of Bloomsbury?'

'Not a bad part. It depends on the price. Did he say the price?'

Ella shook back her long fair hair. 'The prices are I suppose whatever they are.'

'You might miss the room-service,' said Ernst. 'It's convenient to phone down.'

'Frightful meals,' said Ella. 'And by the time you've paid that rent you might as well buy a flat.'

'We can look at these places that Luke has found.'

'If they're not gone already. Luke says Hurley Reed advises to hurry up.'

'Will Luke be helping at Hurley's dinner?'

'Yes. I want to get a dress for the dinner.'

'Oh, I think that dinner's going to be quite a simple affair; nothing grand.'

'Yes, but I want to look nice,' said Ella.

'You always look nice.'

'I think I'll get a new dress for Hurley Reed's dinner,' said Margaret.

'It's nothing grand. Quite simple,' said William.

'Well, I want to look nice.'

She had just made their big double bed. It was a Sunday morning. Very carefully she set out, along the top of the counterpane, a series of worn-out teddy bears and other woolly animals, and three much-handled dolls. William as a bachelor had retained an affection for his old toys, and Margaret, when she realized this, had added a few of her own to the collection.

William's previous girl-friend hadn't liked William's old woollen animal-toys. He had been obliged to hide them in a cupboard all the time they lived together. She was horrified when she found them there; she had thought he had thrown them away. When she parted company from William he brought out his teddy bears, dogs, cats and rabbits again and laid them out along the pillow. It was an enormous relief to him that Margaret not only tolerated the toys but added some tattered dolls of her own. It was in keeping with her goodness and sweetness. He had in the bathroom a plastic duck that swam, quacked and flapped.

'Inspiration from nature', said Margaret, 'is after all, from what you tell me, the basis of the study of artificial intelligence.'

'I never thought of that,' said William. 'Yes, it all ties up with bionics.' He seemed relieved at the thought that his indefatigable feeling for his old cuddly toys might have this serious and respectable connotation.

'I always felt', he told Margaret, 'that they had some sort of sensing mechanisms. Absurd as it sounds, I know, when I hid them in the cupboard I felt I was hurting their feelings.'

'It's so understandable. They have a musky smell, all their smells seem to be a definition of their life.'

'I wouldn't like my colleagues to hear that,' William said. 'But there's a certain something in what you say. It's not scientific of course.'

'Is artificial intelligence a scientific study?'

'Not really. It takes a lot of scientific knowledge to study nature, though, and mimic nature even, and to adapt and apply the way living things work, even with computers. Snakes, moths, birds, even plants, they all tell us something. It's a question of neural conductors, signals, nervous systems.'

'And your toy animals?'

'Symbolic, to be frank, only symbolic.'

'I wonder', said Margaret, 'if there's anything in that practice of sticking pins into dolls?'

'We don't know enough about it,' William said. She was combing her long red hair at the dressing-table mirror while he sat on the new-made bed, watching her.

'I wouldn't like to try it,' said Margaret. 'Why stick pins into the poor dolls?'

He went off to fetch the Sunday newspapers. On the one hand he felt easy after talking to Margaret and on the other hand he felt uneasy. On the whole, he knew very little about her. But then, he reflected, she knew very little as yet about him.

Margaret finished combing her hair, then looked at the bed with its row of dolls and teddies. She quoted to herself a couplet from an ancient Border ballad:

Now speak to me, blankets, and speak to me, bed,
And speak, thou sheet, enchanted web.

11

SHORTLY after the convent was closed down Margaret had gone home to recover her equanimity, as she put it. She complained bitterly about her sisters, who had once again turned on her.

'What did I have to do with Sister Rose's murder?' she said. 'I wasn't there. Nowhere near. I was with Eunice. And what does Eunice say? She says, "It looks very fishy, Margaret. You were mixed up with Granny's murder and now you're mixed up with the murder of the nun." That's so unfair.'

'Take no notice,' said Dan.

'What do you mean, take no notice? She says I'm not to go and visit her any more, she's afraid for her squalling brat. She didn't say squalling brat, of course, she said darling Mark. And then, that very day, when I get back to the Convent of Good Hope, who should ring me up but Flora and that husband of hers, the anal-compulsive bureaucrat.

Do you know what she said? She said there had been too many unfortunate incidents, starting from my schooldays.'

'So there have been,' said Dan. 'Nobody's blaming you.'

'Oh, aren't they; oh, aren't they? I would like to know, I said to Flora, how you think I could be involved in the murder of Sister Rose, a complete and harmless nobody who was the assistant to Sister Rooke who at least was a plumber, a somebody.'

'Nobody's blaming – '

'Oh, no? Listen to this. Flora got questioned again by the police. She's furious. They said it was only a matter of routine. That ought to please her a lot, not to mention her ghastly Bert, they are slaves to routine both of them. But no, the police came to their door, and that was enough. All my fault. Only a couple of months ago, perhaps a bit more, they were saying how sorry they were for me. And now, look how quick people can change. It's – '

'Margaret,' said Dan, gazing in despair and confusion at her wonderful complexion and her piled-up dark-red hair, 'Margaret, leave your sisters out of it. Your mother and I – '

'Oh no, oh no,' said Margaret. 'Mother is terrified. She's inclined to take their part. She is terrorized altogether. And you know it.'

'What can I do? There is no proof against you,

Margaret. There never has been any proof.' Oh God, he seemed to be saying there has always been everything except the proof. He had a small red silk handkerchief tied round his neck, a light brown shirt.

And she answered, 'The Mother Superior made a clear confession.'

In came her mother, Greta, in a pale mauve jersey, a pale fawn skirt and pearls; but nothing could make her look distinguished, which would not have mattered in the least if only she had been friendly. Instead, Greta was frightened. She looked at Margaret with a look that said, What, what, have I begotten?

It might have been strange that they had neither of them, Greta nor Dan, asked themselves this question at least ten years ago, when the unexplained deaths by violence began. But it was not strange. The previous deaths had not drawn public attention as the last two had. Therefore, being more or less feeble, they had taken the previous deaths into their minds only, and stored them away until further notice. Now that the two public occasions had occurred, further notice had likewise happened.

Margaret's best friend at school had jumped into a lake in the school grounds, had swum for it, got caught in some reeds and had drowned. The lake was in a private area, forbidden the girls. Margaret said she saw her friend struggle, having been drawn to the spot by her cries, but was too far away to help. Everyone said what a dreadful thing it had been for Margaret, aged twelve, to witness. Her parents were advised not to mention the incident again. They found another school for Margaret. It was near Hawick on the Borders of Scotland.

Here she was taken to tea in a teashop in the town by one of the teachers as a treat. It was this teacher's habit to take the girls out one by one for a treat. Only, on this occasion the teacher disappeared. She left her gloves on the table, took her bag and went, apparently, to the ladies' room. Margaret waited a long time, over an hour. She then applied to the owners of the tearoom who investigated the ladies' room without success and telephoned the school. No sign of the teacher, a woman in her early thirties whose home was in Staffordshire. It was an unsolved mystery. The papers were full of it for a time, the district was combed by the police and their dogs. Nobody had the slightest clue what had happened to Miss Dewar. Had she said anything special to Margaret before she left the table? 'No, nothing special at all. She ordered the tea and then she went to the bathroom.'

'And you just waited doing nothing?'

'I drank the tea, it was getting cold, and I ate two biscuits. Then I asked the teashop lady to look in the ladies' room as it seemed a long time.'

At that time Magnus was in one of his good periods and on the Sunday he came to his brother's house for lunch and to spend the afternoon. It was only four days after the teacher's disappearance and the search for her was still on.

'It's so bad for young Margaret,' said Greta. 'She's impressionable. What a thing to happen!'

'Such a nice woman, too,' said Magnus.

'Well, you can't tell from a photograph on the television or in the papers. She's probably bonkers,' said Greta.

'I wouldn't say that,' said Magnus. 'She was highly intelligent and very sweet.'

Dan first noticed Magnus's use of the past tense, then the reflective glaze in his brother's eyes.

'How could you know?'

'I met her when I went to visit Margaret,' said Magnus.

'You went to visit Margaret?' said Greta. 'When was that?'

'A few weeks ago. Lovely school. Beautifully situated.'

'She didn't say,' said Greta.

'Oh, I always believe in visiting young Margaret at school. The other girls are extremely self-sufficient. They're all right. But Margaret's very different. I understand her.'

'Magnus, it's time for you to go back,' said Dan.

All those years ago, and Miss Dewar was never found. It was obvious she had gone somewhere of her own accord, but nobody knew where.

'You didn't say Uncle Magnus had been to see you,' Greta said to Margaret.

'I forgot. He often comes to see me. There's nothing wrong with him when they let him out.'

'And he met Miss Dewar.'

'Yes. You met Miss Dewar yourself.'

Margaret was now beginning to look attractive. It was noticeable to Dan that she had a special affinity with Magnus. She took advice from him. As soon as she had a car she drove off to visit him from time to time at the Jeffrey King hospital. When Magnus came to Blackie House for his Sunday outings he always had a special greeting for Margaret if she was there. He liked to quote the Border ballads, and he did it heartily:

'O where hae ye been, my long, long love,
These seven long years and more?' –
'O I'm come to seek my former vows,
That ye promised me before.'

Dan was frightened; of himself, of Margaret, and of Magnus. Before the other two girls were married, they, too, were afraid of Margaret, but without being aware of it. Flora, the eldest, translated her fear into disapproval and, this not being a straightforward emotion, it took a hysterical turn. She would shriek at Margaret on those Sundays of the school holidays when they both happened to coincide at Blackie House, before the arrival of Uncle Magnus.

'You shouldn't encourage him the way you do. Putting forward your sex. Don't you see his pills have side effects and he's got a sex fixation on you?'

'Effex a fix sexation?' Margaret taunted. And then Uncle Magnus arrived, dressed, even in those days, too loudly; dressed, for instance, in a bright blue Harris tweed coat and bright brown Harris tweed trousers, and, as it might be, a purple tie. There was no knowing what Uncle Magnus might wear.

The second sister, Eunice, three years Margaret's senior, and fearful of Margaret, was timid with her red-haired attractive young sister; she was timid but underhand. Her fear took the form of secret bitchiness so that she seemed to be highly amused when Uncle Magnus greeted Margaret with the verse:

O was it a wer-wolf in the wood,
    Or was it a mermaid into the sea,
Or was it a man or a vile woman,
    My true love that mis-shapit thee?

but later, when Magnus had gone, she said, 'What did he mean by "a man or a vile woman"? Why wasn't the man vile but only the woman?'

'That's the ballad, that's how it goes,' said Margaret.

'Don't take Magnus seriously,' said Dan. 'At best he's an enthusiast for Scottish lore.'

'But you ask his advice,' said Flora.

'Forget it,' Greta said. 'I'm the vile woman of the ballads, all right. But I don't think Margaret's misshapen; far from it. Is she? Now be honest.'

'Uncle Magnus meant it in another sense.'

'Why do you always laugh when he recites like that?' Margaret said. 'You should ask him to his face what he means.'

Eunice became flustered when Margaret spoke like this.

And now, years later, after the murder in the nunnery, when Margaret returned home, both Dan and Greta were frightened, as they had every reason to be. Because Margaret's capacity for being near the scene of tragedy was truly inexplicable in any reasonable terms. If they had been able to see, as, to do them justice, nobody else was capable of seeing, that there was absolutely no link of any rational, physical or psychological nature between Margaret's personal activities and what went on around her, Dan and Greta might have felt a certain consolation. But still they would never have let well alone. One can see their point of view. Whether they understood Margaret or not, they couldn't help waiting with dread for the next disaster.

'There's an affinity with Magnus,' said Dan. 'Perhaps we should keep them apart?'

'Too late,' said Greta. 'You can't stop her going to visit him.'

Dan, enamoured of his daughter, couldn't help fancying that, by contrast with Magnus, he himself stood out to advantage. He was aware that Margaret was now cultivating an exterior sweetness which was really not her own. Why? What was she covering up? – 'I really do think', Margaret had said, 'that it's necessary for one of us at least to visit Uncle Magnus. I don't mind the drive. After all, we should sometimes think of *les autres*, don't you agree?'

Magnus came for the Sunday after Margaret's return from the convent to Blackie House. Certainly she had an affinity with Magnus; it was an old alliance. Uncle Magnus, however, was not unpopular with any member of the family. Although he was decidedly mad, he was by far the least boring of all, which goes a long way with a brother, a sister-in-law and four nieces.

'You should get married,' Magnus said to Margaret when they were alone. 'I've been thinking of it for some time.'

'I know. Do you think I have got the evil eye?'

'Think it? – I know it. It's quite obvious. Even your block-headed parents and sisters have begun to notice.'

'I'll tell you what,' said Margaret, 'I'm tired of being the passive carrier of disaster. I feel frustrated. I almost think it's time for me to take my life and destiny in my own hands, and actively make disasters come about. I would like to do something like that.' She sat on the sofa beside Magnus, tossing back her red hair, rather like a newly graduated student seriously discussing her future with her college tutor.

'Perpetrate evil?' Magnus offered.

'Yes. I think I could do it.'

'The wish alone is evil,' said Magnus with the distant equanimity of a college tutor who has two or three other students to see that afternoon.

'Glad to hear it,' said Margaret.

The next Sunday Magnus arrived in a more manic state than Greta and Dan could usually cope with. The source of supply for his vivid shirts was something that neither Greta nor Dan had been able to fathom. When questioned, Magnus's answers were either vague – 'Oh, the shirts, they come my way.' Or pure lies – 'My shirts? – I just send the orderly to the village shop. They come in all colours.' More recently, it appeared that Magnus had received parcels from Mexico and California as well as from the Charing Cross Road in London. There was no doubt that Magnus's capacity for arranging his own life was formidable. It was only his overwhelming fits of wild and savage mania, lasting sometimes for as much as three weeks, even with the pills, that distinguished him from a normal Scottish eccentric and made necessary his permanence in hospital. But as he only put in an appearance during a more placid mental cycle, many of his contemporaries were convinced there was nothing much wrong with Magnus.

That Sunday his shirt was purple with a scarlet tie.

'Are you thinking of giving a television interview, Magnus?' said Dan.

'You're referring to my shirt. Sheer envy. Look at yourself in your drab sweater from some popular department store. I wouldn't be you if you paid me a fortune to do it.'

Magnus went for a walk with Margaret after lunch. They kicked last winter's leaves on the damp floor of the woods. The smell of spring came to meet them along the path. 'I've made out a list,' said Magnus, producing a folded paper from his pocket, and unfolding it.

'What list?'

'A list of eligible bachelors from rich families for you to marry.'

'A list, a whole list?' said Margaret, taking the paper from his hand.

'You will only marry one, of course.'

'But I don't know these people.'

'You only need know one. If I were you I would pick him out with a pin.'

'And then?'

'Pursue him. There are infinite ways. But, if you

are to have any future, my darling Margaret, married you must be, and married well.'

A few weeks later Margaret was shown into one of the well-planned London offices of Warren McDiarmid, chief executive of the firm McDiarmid & Rice, owners of grocery supermarkets and television stations throughout the south of England, with many affiliates in the business of car-radios, video-cassettes, washing machines, microwave ovens, jacuzzi baths and other commodities that added, almost weekly, a new company to their list of trade enterprises. Warren McDiarmid was the only son of Derwent McDiarmid, the senior partner of this vast commercial empire. Margaret had picked him out with a pin from the list of possible candidates for marriage provided for her by Uncle Magnus. How he had got to know who were the rich, young and unattached bachelors available in the country, was, yes, a mystery; but not so much a mystery when the amount of time on his hands was considered, and, not least, the demonic will and single-minded purpose of the mad. Magnus had money and means to buy all the glossy and gossip-column papers he needed; he could send out for anything he wanted amongst such harmless items. He had radio programmes to listen to, Stock Exchange news to follow, television programmes.

But it had taken him only three weeks to compile, which was certainly an achievement.

When Margaret picked Warren McDiarmid she obtained a photograph of him from a publicity agency and, finding his face bearable, rang up his office and asked to speak to him. She was passed to his secretary.

'I would like to interview Mr Warren McDiarmid,' said Margaret, 'for the *Independent Magazine*.' She had chosen this paper because she had decided that if she was found out they would be nicer about it than the others. 'I'm participating in a series of articles about top yuppies, or very successful young businessmen, and Mr Warren McDiarmid is a must,' Margaret said.

Warren McDiarmid agreed to give her half an hour, between twelve forty-five and one-fifteen. He was just back from Frankfurt.

'How do you travel, Mr McDiarmid?'

'Oh, private jet,' he said. 'One has to, in my field.'

He was about twenty-eight, very shaven and gleaming with after-shave. The trouble was, he didn't once look at Margaret. She might have been a squat, fat woman of sixty instead of a slender tall girl in her twenties with wonderful long red hair. He was looking at a place slightly to the left of the wall opposite his desk, where a classical seascape that had a definite Sotheby's look had been hung.

Perhaps he was wondering if the firm had bid too high.

'And do you enjoy being successful, Mr McDiarmid?'

'Oh yes, rather, it gives one another dimension, especially if one can have a free hand as frankly one does in my case.'

'Have you personal plans for the future? – I believe you're unmarried?' said Margaret.

He looked at his watch, round, flat, gold, as it was, while he replied: 'They always ask one that. Marriage. There's no hurry for one to marry of course. On the other hand, inevitably of course in time one will marry and have children.'

Margaret scribbled in what she hoped looked like shorthand which, in fact, she had no knowledge of. 'And do you enjoy living in London, or do you prefer the country?'

'Well, of course in London one lives on the job. But if one has a place in the country, especially in the deep country, Devon, Norfolk, Scotland, it's a damn good thing for one to get away for the weekend and fish, shoot, whatever.'

'And you prefer Devon to Scotland? Or Norfolk? Which would be your choice?'

'In my case one has places in all three.'

(Scribble, scribble . . .)

'Do you like music, Mr McDiarmid?'

'Oh, one goes to Covent Garden, Glyndebourne, when time permits. And now Miss Murchie – '(he had got her name right!) – 'I'm afraid I have to go. One is so much under pressure. My secretary will pass you to my press and publicity agent who I'm sure will fill you in with anything else you want to know. Delighted to have met you.'

Margaret wondered if perhaps later, he would say to himself, 'What a fool I was not to ask that girl to dinner!' She wondered; and would never know the answer. She was lodging in a hostel. There, she threw away her notes, took out Magnus's sheet of paper, smoothed it on the table in her room, shut her eyes and stuck in another pin.

12

MARGARET was disappointed when the pin fell between two names on the list. She would have preferred a straightforward message. She went north to visit Magnus in his hospital and to make a report.

Magnus was quite horrified to hear that the young magnate Mr Warren McDiarmid had not responded to Margaret's charms. He was indignant.

'You are so young, so radiant, and with your colouring, and you're, so how shall I say? – moist and dewy. How could he resist?'

'You know, Uncle Magnus, you are really somewhat cut off from the way things go. With men like McDiarmid there's no such thing as irresistible as business deals. He said he left the house at five every morning to be at his desk at five-thirty to do three hours before eight-thirty. That means he gets up out of his bed at four-thirty, or does he never take a shower and a cup of coffee in the morning?'

'He'll blow his brains out,' predicted Magnus. 'One day when things get too hot for him he'll take a gun and blow out his brains, rest assured, my dear. He is no man for you. How old is he exactly?'

'Twenty-eight, twenty-nine.'

'To think that I was just over forty when I was reprimanded for streaking over Chelsea Bridge. Believe me, I wasn't too old even at forty. We used to take off our clothes and we used to streak, that's what we used to do. And now this imbecilic young magnate sits there looking at his watch, you are eating up his precious time, and time is money. Talk to my press agent, he says. No, Margaret, no, I'm sorry. He'll blow his brains out. Probably he's embezzled a fortune.'

'Well, now,' said Margaret. 'I closed my eyes and jabbed with the pin. The damn thing fell on a space between two names: William Damien and Werther Stanhope.'

'In my opinion Stanhope would be the better match. He trades with Japan.'

'What does he trade?' said Margaret.

'Know-how,' said Magnus. 'Know-how is a prime commodity. The trouble with Stanhope, he's rather tiny. Of course, small men can have power. Terrific power. Personally, I'm afraid of small men, and for a Murchie, that's saying something. But on the other hand they do seem to like tall brides.'

Margaret enquired about William Damien. 'Now he,' said Magnus, 'now he . . .' Magnus opened the door to a small cupboard underneath the television in his sitting-room. From it he extracted a bottle labelled 'The Tonic: *three tablespoons a day with water*'. He poured himself a drink of the liquid, good malt whisky as it was, and continued his discourse. 'Damien is a scientist. Nice and tall for you, my dear. He is not rich himself, but his mother is an Australian business-woman of fabulous means. Mrs Hilda Damien owns newspapers, department stores, and all that goes with them. William has no head for business. He lives modestly, but he is the heir. Now you fix your eye on little Stanhope, he is a clear case of an eligible bachelor, something of a playboy by reputation, but obviously ripe to settle down. He's thirty-two, never been married before. Obviously, you would have to strike quickly with Stanhope before he's snapped up. But William Damien – well, he has some sort of a liaison going, but according to gossip it will break up before long. They are not suited, always having wild rows. If you could catch him, then of course later you could take care of the mother. Now it's time for my snooze.'

His eyes were shut before Margaret had left the room. She took out a comb from her bag, combed her long hair in front of the mirror, and went to the door. Just as she was leaving Magnus opened his eyes and said, sleepily, 'At school I was good as Lady Macbeth. It could be in the family.'

When she had left the Jeffrey King nursing home

she drove to turreted Blackie House. 'I'm exhausted,' she told her mother. 'Flying around the country like this. I have to be back at the office nine-thirty Monday morning. Eunice and Flora never think of visiting Uncle Magnus. No sense of *les autres*. And now look how they've turned on me. First they blamed me for being mixed up in Granny's death; next they were sorry for me; now I'm to blame for Sister Rose's death. I wasn't anywhere near those deaths, those murders.'

'It's just unfortunate,' Greta said. 'Why don't you give up your job and have a holiday?'

'I've got rather a good job at the moment,' Margaret said. 'And I like London.'

'But you might meet a nice young man. I'm sure you could invite some young people here. Sooner or later you'll meet Mr Right.'

'You mean, get a husband like Flora's, a husband like Eunice's?' said Margaret in her melodious voice. 'Let me tell you I find both Bert and Peter infinitely boring. If they were my husbands I'd tip prussic acid into their tea.'

'I wish you wouldn't talk like that,' said Greta, busying her hands with plumping up the cushions. 'Even for a joke.'

Margaret's job in the publicity office of the petrol company in Park Lane was mainly to do with research into the history of sales and auctions of

[154]

the famous paintings which the company purchased from time to time. It was not very complicated. Mainly she obtained, or consulted in libraries, the catalogues of sales and ownerships as far back as could be ascertained. Her colleagues were friendly. The married ones asked her to dinner. There was one unmarried man who took her to a discothèque from time to time; one married man who wanted to touch her, to sleep with her, all the time. It was when Margaret said something soulful about *les autres* that one of the girls in the office said, 'I've heard that before.'

'Oh, it's a French movement.'

'No, but I've heard it on the television. Someone awfully like you was talking about the philosophy of *Les Autres*. I've always thought that it was right to think of others, be considerate and that.'

'Was it a religious programme?' said Margaret.

'Yes, I think it was. Some nuns.'

'Oh, I remember that show,' said Margaret.

Her time was mostly occupied in following William Damien's movements from a safe distance. 'Safe' meant that she left her car at certain hours in the nearest car-park and walked around the block where he lived in a four-storey modern building. She calculated the position of his windows from the names on the street intercom. The very fact that she was in no way a professional sleuth, only a beginner, was very much in her favour. Any blunders she might make – and, indeed, did make

– precluded any probability that she was in fact checking William's movements.

He never even noticed her. As it happened, and it was not so strange that it did happen, since the name Damien spoke for itself whereas William was fairly obscure, someone in Margaret's office was related to a couple who not only knew William but knew 'who he was'. That is to say they knew that William was heir to a vast fortune.

It had come about that a minor French painter of the turn of the century called François Rose, whom nobody had heard of, had been promoted by the auction rooms some months ago. The petroleum company for whom Margaret worked had it in mind to buy a François Rose depicting several bunches of luscious grapes piled on the bulbous belly of a reclining nude woman. Margaret was given the task of investigating its sales history. She found that it was the property of an Australian collector, Hilda Damien, who was putting the painting up to auction as she couldn't stand it any more. Margaret's assistant piped up: 'My sister May and her husband are great friends with her son William. You know, he has a job and maintains himself on his own pay.'

This, Margaret knew already. But she was able, through this girl, sister of May, to fill in a great many gaps that Uncle Magnus's information had left open wide. With her assistant, Margaret was casual, even scornful: a sure way of eliciting more insistent information. 'Look,' said Margaret, 'I'm not here to study or consider the habits or the characters of the sons of the owners of paintings that the company is going to buy, maybe. And it's a big maybe. All I want to know is what Hilda Damien paid for the picture.'

It was not all Margaret wanted to know. The son, apparently, had arranged the original deal, two years ago at least.

'Is he married?' Margaret demanded of her helper, as if it was all in the day's work.

'No. He's living with a girl.' Margaret's assistant could not contain herself from this moment on. 'They've been living together a year or two, but it's no good. They have fearful rows. It's a love-hate relationship.'

'She loves his money but hates him?' Margaret suggested vaguely, meanwhile sorting out something in her handbag.

'Really, he has no money. The mother doesn't give him any, nothing at all. He has to live on his pay. Sometimes they're quite hard up. His girl-friend has to contribute to the expenses. I think she's going to quit. In fact May says she's going to quit. There's something odd about him, besides. Something childish – oh, God save us from that sort.'

Margaret found the college where William was employed on research. She knew the day when, finally, his girl flounced out, with two suitcases in the vestibule of the flats, waiting for a taxi, getting the driver to heave them into the taxi, and up there at the parted curtain of the window watching them drive away, was William. The girl didn't come back. Margaret waited three weeks.

'The Damien boy and his fiancée have had a bust-up,' was one of the statements in a shiny gossip column.

Margaret now followed him all over the place, and she wound up in Marks & Spencer's fruit section.

'Be careful,' she said, 'those grapefruits look a little bruised.'

He looked at her, then he looked at the grapefruit and then he looked at her again. 'So they are, thanks,' he said. He was enchanted by the red-haired beauty with her sexy prominent teeth, who stood beside him, so ready to edge away. She thought him all right to look at provided he didn't put on more weight.

They were married within four months.

Margaret went to visit Magnus shortly after her return from her honeymoon.

'Did you see in the paper about little Werther Stanhope, that he shot himself?' said Magnus.

'You predicted Warren McDiarmid,' she said, kicking off her bright blue shoes, part of her bridal trousseau; they weren't very comfortable. She wore a bright pink dress which Magnus had told her was just right for her colouring. 'Warren

McDiarmid', he now said, 'or Werther Stanhope, what difference does it make? All right, I slightly erred. So far. Perhaps McDiarmid's day of reckoning will come, it is bound to come. You know, if you had married Stanhope instead of Damien you would at this moment be a wealthy widow instead of a wife of a poor man with a rich mother. However, you've done not badly, so far. How do you propose to rid yourself of Hilda Damien?'

'I will bide my time,' said Margaret.

'Perhaps your evil eye will be enough,' said Magnus. 'Only think about it, concentrate enough, and something will happen to her.'

'I don't think you understand how I feel,' she said. 'I want to actively liquidate the woman. Compared with the evil eye, what I have in mind is just healthy criminality. Fortunately I don't like her.'

'Providers are often disliked, often despised.'

'She isn't even a provider. Very limited and such a know-all. Comparatively stingy, too.'

'Here in Scotland,' said Magnus, 'people are more capable of perpetrating good or evil than anywhere else. I don't know why it is, but so it is. That gives you an advantage. For myself let me remind you of Judith and what she did to Holofernes. Pass me the Bible.'

Margaret got ready to go. 'It needs more planning than you think,' she said.

Magnus was reading: 'And approached to his

bed, and took hold of the hair of his head – '

'Plans. We should make plans,' said Margaret.

'And she smote twice upon his neck with all her might, and she took away his head from him.'

'Hilda's coming next week. We have a dinner party on Thursday, then Friday night or Saturday morning I want to drive her up to St Andrews with William. Maybe you could come to Blackie House for the Sunday? We could take her for a walk in the woods, Uncle Magnus.'

'Where is she staying in London?'

'The Ritz.'

'To be perfectly honest,' said Magnus, laying aside his holy book, 'I don't want personal trouble. We've had enough bloodshed, if that's what you mean.'

'Between the two of us', Margaret said, 'we could arrange an accident.'

'Impossible,' said Magnus. 'No guarantee, ever, of success. Too risky.'

'All those suspicions have fallen on me,' said Margaret. 'Why shouldn't I really do it? I'm tired of being made to feel guilty for no reason. I would like to feel guilty for a real case of guilt.'

'Generally speaking,' said Magnus, 'guilty people do not feel guilty. They feel exalted, triumphant, amused at themselves.'

'That's fine. I'd like that.'

'Like it or not,' Magnus said, 'destiny might do it for you.'

She said, 'You'd better think of something before Sunday the 21st or I'll never come here and visit you again. That's final. Do you think I enjoy coming here?' She slipped on her blue shoes, grabbed her coat and went out. She put her head round the door a moment later. 'The ground is slippery with all this rain. Push her in the pond. *You* know how it's done,' she said, and left.

Magnus took a swig of his drink and looked out of the window where there was a marvellous purple and orange sunset. A male nurse came into the room to settle Magnus into his bed. 'All that', said Magnus, indicating the view, 'can be read about in detail in various novels by Sir Walter Scott. Nobody can do sunsets like Scott.'

'That's a fact,' said the nurse.

>:> 13 <:<

ANNABEL said to Roland, 'I'm so glad that man has left.' She was referring to Roland's flatmate, the journalist, who had departed to live with his girl-friend.

'It makes a difference economically,' Roland said. 'Otherwise I like being alone. One can think.'

'There is something for you to think about,' Annabel said. He was just recovered from his 'flu and had invited Annabel to supper at his flat. He had decided to prepare the supper himself, Annabel was not to do anything. The shopping had already been done by his household helper who came three times a week, and now Roland paddled, drink in hand, in and out of the sitting-room where Annabel was relaxing with her vodka martini. She told Roland how she had remembered the television show where she had seen the image of Margaret which corresponded to the press photograph. 'She was in a convent, and there were some shots of her going along Victoria Street on a motor-bike, and some others in a hospital where she was sick-visiting. I arranged a re-run.'

'Are you sure it's the same one? What name?'

'They didn't give her name. Let me see that photograph and I'll tell you if it's the same girl.'

Roland produced the photograph and left Annabel while he went to see to his stove. A thought dawned on him. He turned down the gas and came back. 'Annabel,' he said. 'That nun programme – I remember it. I saw a bit of it and it was hilarious. But do you know there was a sequel. One of the nuns was murdered, there in the convent or in the convent-yard, whatever they call it; nobody was arrested. They couldn't find the murderer. An elderly nun, very dotty, confessed but nobody believed her. I remember well. They thought it was a man, a strangler. I remember they said if he was left-handed he approached from behind, right-handed he came from the front. They knew by the marks on her neck.'

'But that's another murder that the Murchie girl's been mixed up in. If it is the Murchie girl.'

'I can find out if it's her,' said Roland.

'So can I. But from the photograph I'm almost sure it's the same one. What was she doing in the convent?'

'Repenting,' said Roland.

'She's a nut case, obviously,' said Annabel.

'What makes you think so?'

'Just something about the circumstances and something about her.'

'Well, we'll see for ourselves on Thursday at Hurley's dinner.'

They sat down to eat. Lamb chops, peas, and salad. Claret. 'We should tell Hurley,' said Roland.

'You've been dying to tell Hurley since you found out about the first homicide. Don't you think he probably knows already?'

'No, I don't.'

She let a pause go by. 'Neither do I,' said Annabel. 'But what difference does it make? Presumably her husband, young Damien, knows all about her.'

'I wonder,' said Roland very blandly, at the same time pouring wine into their glasses. 'Perhaps he knows hardly anything about her.'

'In that case,' Annabel said, 'you absolutely must keep your big mouth shut, Roland. It would be positively bitchy of you to spread stories about the girl's past. And we are presuming that the nun and Margaret Murchie are the same girl.'

'I can check,' Roland said.

'So can I. But not a word to Hurley, remember,' Annabel said. 'It would look bad. You shouldn't give a gossipy impression, really, Roland; try not to.'

The next morning Annabel checked the BBC files. Yes, the Margaret Murchie of the murdered grandmother was the same as one of the girls in the fatal nunnery.

Roland rang her to tell her the same fact and to add more fruits of his simple investigation: an interview with Eunice in a women's glossy paper referred to Margaret's misfortune at being subject to questioning in two previous cases while she was still at school, one, where a girl was drowned in a pond under her very eyes and the other, where a schoolmistress she was having tea with went to the ladies' room and disappeared for ever. 'There's something about Margaret,' Eunice was reported as saying. 'I'm really sorry for her, as you can't help feeling it, but you don't want your children to get caught up in it.' She refused to be more precise. ('Are your children afraid of Margaret?' – 'No, darling Mark is only a baby.')

Flora and Bert were interviewed together. Bert cautioned the interviewer about the laws of libel and the limits of the law which he himself spoke within. The facts, he said, were isolated from each other. Margaret was not the only witness to the unfortunate occurrences. Flora said, 'My sister is naturally very down to earth. As you know the earth is magnetic. So Margaret attracts people like the press and the television. Her hair is naturally red. There is nothing at all to prove anything against her. I hate it when the police come here to interrogate us. We have nothing to hide.'

Roland read these paragraphs out to Annabel. It

occurred to Annabel he was over-excited. She could understand his being amused or appalled in some ways, but she didn't like that tone of garden-fence gossip, that catty spite that would take hold of him occasionally. 'Roland, do keep it to your-self,' she said. 'You do know what I mean. It could only do you harm for you to go round repeating all this.'

'But isn't it *awful*?' he said.

'It's a mystery, nothing really to do with us.' She made the excuse that someone else was waiting to talk to her on the line; then thought about Roland with a sort of despair.

After that, she began to think over the story of Margaret Murchie. On an impulse she rang the studio, which was in the same building as her office, where the film was being made about an artist with Hurley Reed as adviser. He was expected later in the morning. Annabel left a message to call her back. Annabel had always been rather tactful and ready to render good services to all around her. But of late, with the boredom of daily life, the absence of a steady man-friend, and above all her helpless devotion to Roland, she had become easily exasperated. She longed deeply to tell Hurley Reed all she had found out about Margaret Murchie, hoping mainly that he didn't know already but in any case that they could discuss it. Anything was better than nothing. And the rain was pouring down mercilessly outside the window.

Annabel and Hurley met for a lunch-time sandwich and a drink in the hotel bar across the way. To Annabel's satisfaction Hurley was amazed at the story. 'I myself', he said, 'felt there was something odd about the girl. Chris doesn't believe for a minute she met William Damien by accident. Of course, one doesn't want to interfere, it's nothing to do with us, basically. It's only that I hope Hilda Damien's all right.' He said this with a little laugh.

'Oh, after all, the girl herself was never accused of anything,' Annabel said. 'Of course, when there's madness in the family . . .' Her act of gossip had actually made her feel better. She went on to talk to Hurley about her proposed television documentary of his life and work. 'I hope', she said, 'we could include Charterhouse.'

'As you know, I think a butler's out of place when you're dealing with art,' Hurley said.

'Maybe so,' said Annabel. 'From the psychological point of view, though, there is always the appeal of devotion. If you are shown with a devoted servant or a devoted friend, that somehow appeals; it shows that you inspire devotion.'

'Oh, Charterhouse hasn't been with us for long. I don't know about devotion. Chris is devoted to me, she must be or she wouldn't put up with me as she does. And I'm devoted to her.' But his thoughts were not on any television programme.

He said he had to go, and kissed Annabel; 'See you Thursday night.'

Hilda was on her way to London from Australia. She intended to settle the flat in Hampstead, her wedding present to William and Margaret, and install their surprise bonus of the newly acquired painting by Claude Monet of which all Hilda knew as yet was that it was a joyful view of the Thames painted in 1870.

She enjoyed these long flights to England. One could forget business, read, sleep, relax and dream. With only six first-class passengers on this flight one could have plenty of attention. Almost too much.

Across the aisle was a white-haired healthy-looking man, not essentially unlike herself, but in a decidedly masculine cast, so that the likeness would not have been apparent to a casual observer, although their suitability as companions on the voyage was somehow evident. He came from the same type of highly financed and good-natured people as Hilda.

They gave each other a polite small smile when the steward came round offering drinks.

'Do you like flying?' said the man. His voice was American or Canadian.

'I do, in fact. It's a relaxation,' said Hilda. 'I used to be afraid of flying but I got over it.'

'One does. Best not to think about it. Destiny is destiny, after all. Just relax, as you say. At least, there's nothing we can do, so we might as well enjoy it.'

'I believe in destiny,' said Hilda.

On the phone to Chris when she was settled into her rooms at the Ritz, she said:

'I met a charming man on the plane, a widower. Guess who he is, he's Andrew J. Barnet of the construction and engineering people. Really so nice. It made my journey. He's in London a few days and we're having dinner on Friday.'

'But we'll see you Thursday, Hilda. You'll look in after dinner, won't you?'

'After dinner. With Margaret and William out of the way at your house I want to take advantage of their absence to take in the Monet. What a surprise! I hope they appreciate it.'

'What's it like?'

'I haven't seen it myself, yet.'

'Are you busy tonight?' said Chris.

'No, are you? Come here and dine with me.'

'Have a rest,' said Chris.

'I'm not tired.'

'I'll look in after dinner. Perhaps Hurley will come. We want to talk to you.'

'Me, too.'

When Chris and Hurley arrived at the Ritz to see Hilda they found her admiring an enormous bunch of flowers of every conceivable kind, in season and out of season.

'How lovely,' said Chris. 'Compliments of the management?'

'No, my travelling companion.' Hilda seemed very amused, almost laughing at herself.

'Do William and Margaret know you're in London?' Chris said.

'Not yet.'

'What do you feel about Margaret?'

'You know how I feel. I don't trust her. There's something odd. I'll never believe she met William in Marks & Spencer's fruit section by chance.'

'People meet people by chance. You met your admirer who sent these flowers by chance,' Hurley said.

'Let's hope it was lucky chance,' said Chris.

'I don't believe Margaret's particular story, that they met by chance,' said Hilda. A little later when they had settled with their coffee and drinks this clever woman said, 'What have you got to tell me?'

'Nothing,' said Hurley, the whole scene appearing too absurd to be real. Here he was with Chris, come to pass on hearsay about Hilda's new daughter-in-law. It was altogether too low. Chris kept quiet, too. She followed his feeling. It was the following morning on the phone that Hilda got the new information. Chris told her as neatly and briskly as possible.

'But', Chris added, 'just because she's been

mixed up in all those disasters doesn't mean – '

'It's been going on inside me that she's not right,' said Hilda. 'I've been wondering if all mothers-in-law are like that.'

'I think, up to a point, most of them are,' Chris offered. It was apparent she was very embarrassed when it came to openly deprecating a newly married girl to her mother-in-law.

However, before the conversation ended she said, 'Be careful, Hilda.'

'I promised to go to St Andrews on Saturday morning to stay with the Murchies. Do you think I shouldn't go? Should I make an excuse?' said Hilda.

'I don't know. Just be careful, Hilda.'

'Luke,' said Ella, 'you're not looking so well, these days. Are you studying too hard? – All those evening jobs etcetera etcetera etcetera.'

'I jog every morning,' Luke said.

'My God, you don't! How much energy do you have to spend?'

'Energy to burn,' said Luke.

'But you don't look so well,' said Ella.

Luke was on his way out with a tote-bag. He had come to collect some things he had left behind the last time he stayed at the flat. It looked very much as if Luke was leaving for good.

'Who gave you that marvellous watch?' said Ella.

'A gentleman gave it to me.'

'You can't be studying seriously,' Ella said. 'It's not possible. You have a career ahead of you, a brain. You should give up your gentlemen. You must have dropped out from your studies.'

'Must I?'

'Almost certainly,' she said.

'Have you decided on a flat?' said Luke, as if to remind her that he had not neglected her recently.

'Yes, Luke, I think I'm settled on the second one. Bloomsbury is rather attractive. I'll let you know as soon as it's settled. It was good of you to find it.'

He lifted his tote-bag and went to the door.

'See you on Thursday,' he said.

'Thursday?'

'The dinner at Mrs Chris Donovan's,' he said.

'Oh yes, of course. You're helping out.'

He left in the haste that denoted other, more important, business.

Luke was gone. He was away, out of her range of influence, out of Ernst's orbit. They had as good as lost Luke, both of them. 'A gentleman' had given him the watch. Why, she wondered, did he waste his time doing odd jobs like serving at table for dinner parties?

Ernst arrived at that moment. She recognized the rattle of his key in the lock that was special to him. 'I just saw Luke downstairs,' he said, stroking back his hair.

'Yes, he came to collect some things of his. What did he say?'

'I didn't have a chance to speak to him. He just waved and threw his bag into the car. And he drove off. A Porsche, very expensive and new. I wonder whose it is?'

'Probably his own,' said Ella.

'The world is going mad,' said Ernst. 'He serves at table and flashes about with expensive clothes and a Porsche, latest model. Did you see his clothes?'

'I didn't notice the clothes,' Ella said. 'But there's something wrong.'

'The world is going mad. I've just heard from my office in Brussels today about a simultaneous interpreter who went mad from exhaustion. He interpreted everything wildly wrong at an international meeting. Then he took a knife and went round threatening everybody.'

Ella brought him his drink. 'Simultaneous interpreters have nervous problems,' she said. Perhaps his story referred to Luke. Ernst often said one thing with reference to another. But Ella couldn't see any connection in this case, and didn't care.

>:> 14 <:<

MARGARET had given up her job with the petrol company when she got married. She knew nothing about a painting by Monet having been sold at Sotheby's. In fact she had lost interest in that type of work; it had served her purpose. She stared at Hilda when she came to lunch, the day after her arrival in London.

Hilda's first thought was that Margaret knew about her purchase of the Monet. It had been in Margaret's line of business to know about the sale at Sotheby's. On the other hand, the purchaser's name had been kept secret. Only Hurley and Chris knew she was now the owner.

Everything went through Hilda's head, every suspicion. Hilda chatted while they waited for William to appear for lunch. In the meantime she was aware of her own great prosperity and she thought of Margaret and the waste of life in her past, and she could swear that the way the girl was looking at her meant she was plotting against her.

She remembered the night and two days she had spent at the Murchies'.

'I'm not sure I'm going to manage to come north at the weekend,' she said. 'There are so many business things to see to.'

'Don't say that, please don't say that,' said Margaret in her softest voice. 'William will be desperately disappointed. We were counting on a weekend in the country with you. Mum and Daddy are looking forward to it. They have so little – one has to think of *les autres*.'

Hilda's suspicions were a whirling panic. She couldn't put her finger on it; yes, she could put her finger on it. The Monet, the new painting, Margaret must know it was now Hilda's and had not foreseen that it would be a wedding present for her, for William. Why Hilda, an even-headed woman, should imagine herself to be in danger because of the Monet, merely, can only be explained by the panic that Margaret provoked in her. Destiny, my destiny, thought Hilda. Is she going to poison me? What is she plotting? She is plotting something. This is a nightmare.

Hilda was right. Except that in the destiny of the event Margaret could have saved herself the trouble, the plotting. It was the random gang, through the informers Luke and Charterhouse, of which Margaret knew nothing, who were to kill Hilda Damien for her Monet.

'I could fly up on Saturday,' Hilda offered. 'I'm very tied up before then.'

'Fine,' Margaret said, 'fine.'

William arrived less than fifteen minutes after Hilda. He relieved the tension, but he wondered why his mother looked distracted.

The day of the dinner, 18th October, in the morning, a large van drew up outside Chris Donovan's house in Islington. It was a great consignment of furniture for Hurley Reed that he had told his widowed mother several times not to send. She had just moved to a smaller house near Boston and she had felt the only thing to do with the surplus furniture, practically a houseful, was to ship it to Hurley, her only offspring. Hurley had thought that the last telephone conversation he had with his mother had settled the matter. 'I don't have room for it,' he had said, not once but over and over again. And she, equally, repeated that she couldn't possibly send such good furniture to be sold, it should be kept 'in the family'. 'What family?' he had demanded. His mother knew very well he had been living with Chris all these years, she had even met Chris, it had all been very amicable. But still she couldn't get it out of her head that Hurley 'might get married one day' and need that furniture, those bedsteads, tables, sideboards, hanging cupboards, thick wood and studded-leather chairs, corner cupboards, made of mahogany, walnut, cherry wood. Not to mention the ornamental lamps and the bronze horsemen that Hurley knew had been wont to stand on or hover over these lump-masses of wood. In spite of his pleas, she had shipped them off to Hurley, transit paid; and here was the van taking up nearly all the road, and the moving men descending in their overalls, throwing open the back doors of the van, ready for action.

'Stop!' cried Hurley.

The foreman came forward with his documents. 'Reed live here?'

'That's me,' said Hurley, 'but you don't bring that stuff here. I don't have any room, we're already cluttered.'

'Got to deliver it,' said the man while the other men sauntered round to hear what was going on.

It went on for over half an hour. The traffic in the street slowed down, and Hurley went indoors and telephoned frantically to every storage ware-house in the Yellow Pages. It was half-past twelve before the men were very beneficially persuaded to take their consignment to the warehouse that Hurley had found willing to take his goods at short notice. But even then, he had to lead the van there in his car, and personally pay a deposit.

'It's been one of those days,' said Hurley to Chris when he got back. 'Not a stroke of work done.' They were eating a sandwich lunch which

Corby had prepared. Corby made delicious sandwiches, full of real food, as he called it, not at all like the cafeteria products. Corby's sandwiches and fruit juice constituted Hurley's favourite lunch. Chris laced her fruit juice with vodka.

Charterhouse was out and the daily maid had left. Corby, that skilled Mauritian of Indian origin, put his lean brown face round the door: 'Everything all right?'

'Fine, thanks,' said Hurley.

When he had gone, Chris said, 'Corby's worried.'

'Why? Haven't we settled the menu for tonight?'

'Oh, the food – that's all right. It isn't that. It's Charterhouse. Corby does simply not take to him. He's deeply suspicious but if I ask, suspicious about what, he just shakes his head. He says we should be careful what we say in front of Charterhouse.'

'Careful what we say? What on earth do we say?'

'Of course Mauritius still has a very primitive element, you know. Their witchcraft. They sense things.'

'Perhaps Corby senses right,' said Hurley. If he had not been so worn out by the bureaucratic and other struggles over the furniture consignment of the morning he would have had Corby in, then and there, to question him. 'We shouldn't get too mixed up with their domestic feuds,' he said.

Chris said: 'I told Corby we could have a talk about it tomorrow. I want to get my hair done this afternoon and have a beauty-nap before the dinner.' And she said, 'You know, I don't want to lose Corby after all these years. There could very well be something in what he says.'

Hurley went to his studio to mooch over his work.

In the course of the afternoon Chris received two phone calls. One was from Helen Suzy to say that Brian's daughter Pearl had arrived in London, a last-minute decision, and was sleeping it off. Could Pearl come along and join them after dinner with a couple of friends?

'Yes, of course,' said Chris. 'Delighted.'

The second phone call was from Hilda Damien. 'I'm taking the painting along to the flat, myself, tonight. Yes, it's manageable, with the help of the taxi-driver I hope. There's a lift, of course. The picture is so lovely I'd like you to see it. I'm tempted to keep it for myself.'

'Why don't you?' said Chris.

'I'm sort of superstitious. I bought it for them and they should have it. Chris, I'm really nervous about Margaret after hearing what you've found out.'

'I didn't want to make ill-feeling,' said Chris.

'Ill-feeling, no. Facts are facts. I'm glad to know,

and I did already feel ill-will oozing out of her towards me. Right from the start. It seems to freeze the air between us. William's such a fool, he keeps repeating that phrase, "Be careful, the grapefruit could be bruised," or something like that, which Margaret said to him when they first met in Marks & Spencer's. It's childish.'

'Does he know anything about her past life, or about the Murchies?'

'Honestly,' said Hilda, 'I don't think he knows a thing. She hasn't told him anything, I'm pretty sure.'

'Well, Hilda, I don't think she's committed any crime, after all.'

'She's perfectly innocent, of course, as far as one can gather. But what malign vibes that girl gives out! Do you think she could plot some evil against me? I'm a bundle of nerves. William dotes on her. I don't want to antagonize him by talking behind her back, as it were. That red hair – '

'If I were you,' said Chris, 'I would keep the picture and go right back home. You're a sensible woman, you're a brilliant woman and everybody knows it. Keep right out of their way. I've never known you like this before.'

'And not go to the Murchies' for the weekend?'

'No, not go, definitely.'

'I want to give the young couple the picture, anyway. I'd better do that. It might sweeten her up. A flat in Hampstead and a London painting by Monet, what more can she want?'

The pheasant (*flambé* in cognac as it is) has been passed round a second time and most people have taken a tiny touch of everything, so good to taste, with peas, small carrots, small sausages rolled in bacon, sauté potatoes. Charterhouse has taken round a serving plate, Luke has followed with another. Hurley has served the wine at his end of the table, Chris at hers, helped willingly by Brian and Ernst on her right and left.

There is no more clatter of a serving fork to the floor. The plates have been taken away and now, in the Continental order of serving – cheese before sweet, preferred by Chris, rather than the reverse English order which Hurley likes better – arrives Stilton cheese, salad, not too swiftly, absolutely silently, with very attractive old Wedgwood plates.

While they are talking amongst each other, most of the guests and the two good hosts are, with another part of their minds, thinking of Margaret. To the accompaniment of good food and wine everything seems less drastic, including the position in the world of Margaret with her long red hair and blue beaded dress.

Chris thinks, We can't possibly be involved in a witch-hunt. She's a perfectly attractive girl. 'I do so agree,' she says to her neighbour, Ernst, who has said it would be sheer madness to put your money into the Channel Tunnel.

'Of course,' says Ernst, 'the Channel had to go. Like the Berlin Wall. But investing in the Tunnel is something else again. The maintenance. And the French franc, oh my God!' He is looking at Margaret, wondering where, in Brussels, he could have seen her before. Some night spot? At Antwerp, one of those wonderful restaurants near the docks? Or nowhere? Newly married into the Damien fortune, as he understood. He looks round for Luke and is consoled to see him standing still by the sideboard.

'And there I was. Ten-thirty this morning,' Hurley is telling Ella Untzinger, 'with a houseful of furniture on my hands. That's all I need. So I just said, "Stop. Stop right there. Don't open that van. If you care to step inside the house," I said, "you can see for yourself we have already furniture and to spare." So what do I have to do? I have to spend the whole morning trying to find a place . . .' He is thinking, She wouldn't be bad to paint, if I could get her out of that pre-Raphaelite pose with her spectacular hair and see more of her prominent teeth. I could go back off into portraits, any time. She would be a really good subject if she'd sit still and take off those absurd clothes.

Ella says, 'The thought of moving house is appalling. We're moving to a flat in Bloomsbury and we've decided to be ruthless. Furniture can be an impediment to one's active career, it can actually impede spiritual and artistic development. Beware of furniture, Hurley.' Ella looks over her shoulder to where Luke stands, waiting for his next round of services. Charterhouse has appeared beside him. Ella hears Luke say something about 'Mrs Damien' and, curious, makes an effort to hear the rest. 'She's not here, not the mother. The red-haired one is the young . . . a mistake.' The voice was lost in the other sounds of the room. She is indignant with Luke for having behaved in such an offhand manner the other day. After she and Ernst have set him up, more or less, in London, with advice and meals and drinks and evening jobs to help his university career, he has started to behave like a spoiled brat, a whore. She is thankful, at least, he has turned up tonight and not let her down. But it must be the last time, she is sure it is the last time.

'Venice', Roland is saying to Helen Suzy, 'can often be wonderful in November. The crowds of tourists have gone home. You can also get around quicker. It may just be that some of the museums and galleries are closed down, they say for cleaning or for reorganization and so on but it's only to give the staff a rest. How you go about getting into a gallery that's closed down is, you write a little appeal to the curator at the back of your card and send it in. Have you got a visiting card?'

'No, but Brian has.'

'That will do. So long as they think you're special, they'll let you in. In Venice and in Naples you can do everything if you're special. In between, Tuscany, Umbria, Lombardy, being special is a way to get nowhere. In Rome everybody is special so priorities cancel themselves out; if you aren't in the Vatican your uncle is; if you aren't in a government office you will be next week. Do you speak Italian?'

'No, but Brian does a bit.'

'Well, that's fine. Get him to scribble a few words presenting his compliments to the egregious director of the museum, if it's closed. If the director is not there himself one of his myrmidons will let you in.'

Chris notes with satisfaction that Roland is capably fulfilling his role of 'talking to a tree'; Roland himself is far from thinking that Helen is a tree. What a waste, he thinks, that this slim girl with her boy-short hair should be going to Venice next week with raddled Lord Suzy, an intensive-care case of loquacious boredom. It would be nice, Roland thinks, to take this pretty, flat-chested, boyish gawk round Venice himself. And as for Margaret Damien, she makes him shudder, sitting there with her simper as if she were still a Sister of Good Hope. If I was really bitchy, he thinks, as Annabel supposes I am, I would ask her here and now, quite openly, 'Weren't you attached to that convent where the young novice was killed? – I'm sure I saw you on the television.'

There is a changing of plates at the table. Luke and Charterhouse seem to float, it is a ballet. White sparkling wine is poured into those twinkling crystal glasses which are meant for it. In comes the sweet course which the English in their lunatic way call the pudding, whether it be leaden with suet or fluffy to the last rarity, no matter; on this occasion it is *crème brûlée*. '*Crème brûlée*', observes Annabel, 'is actually a Creole dish.'

'I didn't know that,' says Chris.

'I wish I knew how to make it,' Annabel says. She looks across the table to Margaret, the new bride. 'Can you cook?' she says.

'Only basics,' says Margaret. 'I took a three-week course. And you?'

'When I've got time,' says Annabel, 'and some-one to eat the food with, I like to cook a meal.'

'It's a question of *les autres*,' Margaret says. 'One can't live unto oneself.' She is thinking how much she craves to be back in Scotland with her father looking terrorized through his smoke-glasses into the distance and her mother weakly trying to cope with her horse-racing debts and her menopause; there, Margaret is at home and feels it. She longs for the weekend, the coming Sunday, and sees quite clearly how easily Hilda can go into the pond, a push, with Uncle Magnus kneeling, holding her down. She thinks: What am I doing among these people, what am I doing here? And, while the chatter goes on around her, and William smiles lovingly and a little fearfully in her direction, it is a relief to let her mind dwell with savagery on Hilda. Her brain fills with a verse of a wild ballad:

Awa', awa', ye ugly witch,
   Haud far awa' an' lat me be!
For I wouldna once kiss your ugly mouth
   For a' the gifts that ye could gie.

'Actually,' she says to Annabel, 'I've got the chance to go back to my job, and I think I'll take it.' She describes to Annabel the job at the petroleum company.

'That sounds interesting,' Annabel says. 'What did you do before that?'

'Oh, this and that,' says Margaret, and looks slightly belligerent.

Annabel, thinking of those television shots of Margaret in the convent, holds her peace. A female Jekyll and Hyde, she thinks. And she wonders, What were precisely the crimes of Mr Hyde? One is never really told.

Brian Suzy is saying, 'These thieves actively want us to sit round our dinner tables discussing them. They desecrate our property largely to show off to each other.'

'I thought', says William, 'that they express contempt only when they don't find much to steal.'

'They could have stolen more from me,' says

[187]

Brian. 'But of course we were in the house at the time. The police will get them of course. They're a gang; they generally go where the people are absent.'

They are in the sitting-room with their cups of coffee. Luke swims round with the tray of liqueurs. Helen can see Luke better now. She thinks, What a nice-looking boy.

A trill at the bell. The sound of the front door being opened and, as it seems, a multitude of voices. In then come four young people who seem to be far more than four in all, they are so vibrant and flowing over. Pearl, who is Brian's daughter, is extremely pretty. She has brought two girls and a young man. The girls are all dressed in short dark hanging-rags over very long legs; in their elegance they make the other women in their expensive party clothes look rather frumpy, while the men suddenly feel they have missed the boat. The fourth member of the incoming party is a young man with a black velvet suit, a snowy-white wisp of beard and a snowy-white tuft of hair rising from the front of his head, which is otherwise bald. When they are settled with the fruit juices and other drinks that they want, it emerges that all except Pearl are at an art school and that Pearl, too, is enrolled for an art course next term. The great draw of the evening, for them, is obviously Hurley.

He says to himself, Everyone goes to art school nowadays. There won't be enough walls left to hang their stuff on. But he makes the noises of an avuncular maestro, asking each in turn about their work, their ideas. The young man wants to be polemical but Hurley throws him deftly at every turn. 'Have you seen the Rouault exhibition? – You should see it. It's well worth a trip to Paris.' 'Have you seen those Raeburns, talking of public portraiture – they're on show till November the 8th.' So he steers them away from personal probing, and Chris, catching his eye, knows what he is thinking. He is longing for tomorrow to get back to his studio. She mixes up the guests by moving about herself, a little, from place to place. William looks at his watch. 'I don't expect Mother will be coming, now.' 'Oh, there's still time,' says Hurley, getting up to refill someone's glass. But Chris knows that the party is virtually over.

Hilda arrives at Hampstead at about nine with the picture. It is heavier than she expected but the taximan has come up in the lift to the flat with her, has been duly rewarded and has gone away. Hilda has no intention of hanging the picture. She is going to leave it against any wall of the sitting-room, where William and Margaret can see it when they come in.

She has no opportunity of setting it against any

wall. No sooner has she closed the front door after the departure of the taxi-driver, but three men are upon her. They come along from the kitchen. They are unmasked, recognizable. This is something they have not expected and this is the tragic fact for which Hilda dies. She screams as loud and long as she can. Two of the men, agile and young, take the painting quietly out of the flat, while the third, burly and rather older than the others, smothers Hilda. She is not strangled, as the papers are to give out at first, she is smothered, her head held down hard and firm on the sofa, the man with one knee on her body, until she is dead.

Still, her screams have been heard. Two cars outside have been seen to drive off at a suspicious rate. Two neighbours in the building have called the police.

Before ten o'clock the police have caught the gang for whom they have been looking for weeks; they have found Hilda's body, beyond resuscitation.

Hurley and Chris are saying good-night to their friends when the bell rings.

'Hilda!' says Chris.

It is not Hilda, but a police officer. They have found Hurley's name in her diary: *'Look in after dinner.'*

Hurley stands at the front door with the police-man. Another officer sits outside in the police car, waiting. 'Hilda Damien? Her son is here.' William is staring at the man in uniform.

'They stole a picture. I'm very sorry to tell you that Mrs Damien has been the victim of a misfortune. My condolences. If you wouldn't mind coming along.'

'No, it can't be,' Margaret shrieks. 'Not till Sunday.'

'Chris, look after Margaret. I'll go with William,' Hurley says.

The policeman is looking along towards the kitchen where in the back hall Luke is changing his waiter's coat very hurriedly for his outdoor jacket. 'Where are you going?' the policeman calls out to him.

'Home,' says Luke.

'You're in a hurry.'

'Yes.'

'Well, you're coming with us,' says the officer.

Hurley says to his guests, who stand gasping and exclaiming, 'Good-night, everyone. Please go home.'

From upstairs comes Margaret's wild cry: 'It shouldn't have been till Sunday!'

Next morning Andrew J. Barnet will read in *The Times* that his new friend and fellow-magnate Hilda Damien has been murdered by a gang of house-robbers, fed by domestic informers, who have been active in the wealthy suburbs in the last few weeks.

Andrew Barnet will not at first be able to grasp the fact that he will not be taking her to dinner that evening. He will remember her on the plane, attractive, and so used to wealth and success that everything was easy between them as they talked. Like speaks unto like. He had ordered and sent her the flowers.

He will not now be able to face his working day. He will give instructions to cancel meetings, and will then look in his address book for the telephone numbers of some English friends of whom he will stand in great need. He will want more than anything to talk, to tell them how he had met Hilda Damien.